S T R A Y E R

STRAYER

A Fertile Dirt Studio Series

Charleston, SC
www.PalmettoPublishing.com

Strayer
Copyright © 2021 by Fertile Dirt Studio

All rights reserved

No portion of this book may be reproduced, stored in a retrieval system, or transmitted in any form by any means–electronic, mechanical, photocopy, recording, or other–except for brief quotations in printed reviews, without prior permission of the author.

Hardcover ISBN: 978-1-68515-011-2
Paperback ISBN: 978-1-68515-005-1
eBook ISBN: 978-1-68515-006-8

TABLE OF CONTENTS

Cigarettes, Sharks, and Love · 1
Dreams of the Abyss · 8
Balls, Blood, and Ricky Clark · 13
The Wages of Sin · 26
The Pig Mask · 35
Runaway · 53
Martha · 67
Snares, Seduction and Otis · 75
Claude Fraley and Miss July · 86
Baseball Is Not for Everyone · 94
How They All Unravel · 100
Molly Stover · 121
Truth Is Stranger than Fiction · 126
Hell Town · 144
No Time to Search for Dead Whores · · · · · · · · · · · · · · · 152
Strayer · 161
The Last Act · 169
The Last True Queen · 176
Dead Men See All Things · 181
Hungry Maggots Must Survive · 197
Venezuela · 200

CIGARETTES, SHARKS, AND LOVE

The crisp October air slithered along with the trees as the small branches shook, releasing the last leaves into the night. The darkness gave way to a rust-framed porch lamp that flickered as the wind brushed against the house. Light stretched to his back as he sat facing into darkness and dangling his feet off the edge of the porch. His exhale pushed out smoke as the cherry flickered. The cheap tobacco and dangling feet left his mind to wander as he stared into the darkness. The alley beyond the yard was littered with trash cans and lined with buildings. The quiet stillness of the neighborhood left little to command attention.

Shadow puppets against the wall of the old white porch amused him. However, the generic entertainment could not harbor his thoughts for long. His amusement gave way to the extent of his imagination, filling his mind with many questions. His long brown hair became tangled with the wind as he wrestled it into the collar of his jean jacket. This bargain that he felt he received was worth it. He argued with himself over his decision-making. "I could have been at the drive-in," he mumbled as if there were someone else in the dark to debate.

The answers Tim had provided for himself left him lost in thought. The wind gusted and howled as if to add itself to his personal argument. Finishing off his last drag, he flicked the cigarette into the night, backed up against the wall, and pulled his jacket tight. Taking one last look in the distance to try and see the drive-in lights dancing in the northern sky, he turned his head to look up at the red glow coming from the upstairs window and whispered to himself, "All because of them," before frowning and burying his head into his jacket's raised collar. His hair was left free to whip in the wind. Comfortable enough to let his mind cease all debates, he drifted into calm.

The red glow gave way to her—face down, half covered in layers of blankets and sheets. The bed was a tangled mess tucked in the corner of the room. The other half of her body lay naked, reflecting the red light coming from the top of the dresser. Her long hair resembled strands of cinnamon, almost fluid, flowing out from her crown in all directions. The silence of the room agreed with the ambiance, only broken by the faintness of her breath. This moment of peace seemed frozen in time and lasting. A question finally disturbed the serenity. "Do you love me, Molly Stover?"

The stillness lingered for a bit until repeated. Then, finally, Molly raised her head, brushing the hair from her face, and began to focus her eyes as she looked around the red room. Removing the blankets from her body and rubbing the dampness off her chest as she sat up, she looked in the direction of the hall. "John," she stated as she waited for a reply. Footsteps grew louder from the hall as John emerged into the bedroom. Covered at his waist only by a towel, he walked over to the light switch, turning on the overhead light before turning the red lamp off. "Love," Molly echoed as she squinted in the new white light from above.

John stood at the foot of the bed, narrowing his eyes to mimic her squint. He mocked her as he ran his hand through his hair, pushing the wet strands back away from his forehead. John proceeded to hold his hand on top of his head as he waited for a reply. Finally, deciding to sit on the edge of the bed at Molly's feet, John spoke again. "Yes, Molly Stover. Love. You will be eighteen soon and done with school."

John paused to adjust his towel as he leaned in closer and softened his voice. Then, John repeated the word *love* to Molly again to wait for a response. But instead, Molly sat up and stopped squinting as she looked directly at John and said with a stern voice, "My father would kill you if he ever found out about us. I would end up getting sent to live somewhere terrible, like Indiana with Aunt Betty on her farm."

John pleaded again, "Molly, I love you. Who cares about your dad? You will soon be an adult and won't need his approval." Molly paused as she looked directly at John's face and sighed as she placed her hands on his shoulders and began to massage. "Construction can barely pay for this broken old house and take care of you; how are we supposed to live?"

John sat silently on the bed, lost in thought, as Molly stopped the massage and moved out of the tangle of blankets to make her way down the hall. Molly stopped and turned at the head of the hallway while looking back at John as he slipped down flat onto the bed, stirring to get comfortable. Then, Molly flipped the light switch, making the room dark, before heading to the bathroom.

Molly gathered her clothes from the bathroom floor into a pile as her mind recounted the eve's events. Molly paused at her reflection in the mirror above the sink. Feeling unsettled, she placed her clothes on the top of the vanity and bent to start the shower. Molly waited for the steam to build from the hot flowing water. Her emotion controlled her as she stepped into the hot, steamy shower. What is love, and what about her dad? Could her parents even begin to understand how she felt? How did she even know how she felt? This conflict left her staring at the drain with the water pouring over her head. She began to scrub her naked body, washing off the smell of sex as her mind swirled with thought. Her brother would be left behind to deal with Mom and Dad. What trouble would he encounter for knowing about this secret?

What would her future hold with John? He was older. Would he understand her needs? The shower seemed to last forever but stopped as Molly stepped out, still with confusion. Her mind cluttered as she dried up after turning off the water. Molly proceeded to get dressed and slip back into her school clothes. She carefully fixed herself to hide the fact that she was fucked.

Satisfied with her effort, Molly made her way down the hall into the dark bedroom. Finding John's forehead with what little light the window brought, she kissed him very gently as he slept. Then she disappeared quietly from the room, walking softly down the stairs and into the living room. Molly paused for a moment to look back as the guilt of her harsh words toward John made her heart sink. "Maybe I love you too," Molly whispered as she turned and walked out into the autumn night.

The full wrath of the cold wind whipped across the yard. Stepping off the porch, she shivered a bit as she whispered, "Tim, are you still here?" She investigated the darkness, and over her shoulder, she heard a rustle. Tim appeared beside her.

"Are you ready?" Tim asked as he stretched and shook himself to get ready for the walk home.

Molly looked at Tim and suggested he could have waited inside instead of hanging out in the cold. Tim responded by laughing and humping the air. Molly stopped walking, turned, and looked at Tim with a scowl on her face. Tim gestured with a hump of the air as if they were frequently intimate. Tim accompanied his affair with the wind by some high pitch moaning. Tim stopped as Molly handed him a pack of cigarettes. Tim smiled before stuffing the cigarettes into his inner jacket pocket and began to walk once more into the night. "I am so going to hell for that one," Molly said as she frowned. "I hope you have a plan in case Dad is up!"

Tim looked at Molly and smiled before spouting, "Oh, I have a plan!"

Molly walked as Tim kept pace. They crossed from alley to the street and into another alley. They changed direction from the riverfront and downtown, entering their neighborhood. Tim spoke up with a hint of sarcasm in his voice. "This is the last time I do this, Molls. All of this lying to Dad is going to catch up to us."

Molly stopped walking long enough to turn to Tim and halt his progress. She replied, "I know, Tim, and I think Mom already knows, and you are right; Dad pays attention." Molly continued as she smiled at Tim. "But cigarettes aren't free, and we both have our secrets from Dad, so let's hurry before we get ourselves into trouble!"

Tim looked back at Molly and smiled as he removed the cigarettes from his jean jacket and shoved them down the front of his pants, pulling down the front of his flannel shirt to cover the odd bulge just behind his button and top zipper. Proceeding to walk on to Kennedy Street with their view home, Tim slowed his pace. He looked at all the houses he passed, looking for a glimpse of his neighbors.

He saw Mrs. Roads sitting by the window in her white gown with her hair up in rollers. She sat by the window, and the lamplight was absorbed by what looked like a newspaper. The next house was Mr. Stevenson. He sat in his recliner with his back toward the window. The television flickered blue light in his dark living room. Then there was home as Tim cut through the yard with Molly close behind. Stepping up to the enclosed porch and gently opening the screen door, they made sure not to slam it. They both made it to the front door.

Tim turned the knob and pushed the creaky door open, leading to the living room. Molly immediately ran up the stairs across the carpet to the railing and stairs in front of the entrance. Tim gently closed the front door and began to follow Molly before being stopped by a deep voice from somewhere behind him. "Tim," the voice called as he immediately stopped on the stairs.

"Yes, Dad," Tim replied, turning to travel back down the steps and onto the carpeted landing.

"How was the movie?" his dad inquired as he lay on the couch in front of the television.

A pizza box and a series of empty beer bottles lined the floor. Tim smiled and held his hands over his head to measure an object. "Huge shark, Dad, and it ate people—lots of people, even a boat," Tim explained as he motioned with his hands and bent at the knees to emphasize a boat sinking. His dad's firm demeanor turned into a half sober chuckle followed by a bit of a smile underneath his thick black beard before he told Tim good night. He got up to turn off the television, returning to his resting position on the couch and closing his eyes. Tim sized up the moment and ran up the stairs where Molly stood grinning to approve his performance. Tim smiled before telling his sister good night and turning to walk into his room.

―

Closing the door behind him, Tim proceeded to remove the cigarettes from the front of his pants. He turned on a lamp by the bed before kneeling to pull up a loose board on the floor. Tim placed the pack among a stack of red cigarette packages, carefully placing the board back into position. Tim rose to his feet, removing his jean jacket and putting it on a pile of clothes on his dresser before placing his boots at the foot of the bed. Tim peeled off the layers of clothes, tossing them into a corner.

    He stripped entirely down to his white underwear. Tim proceeded to slowly open his bedroom door to see if his sister was in the hallway. Running down the hall and sliding his feet before stopping at the open bathroom entrance, Tim slammed the door before turning to shake off the last of the cold night. He finished by washing his hands, splashing water on his face, and quickly brushing his teeth before opening the bathroom door, shutting off the light, and running down the hallway.

    He slid on the hardwood, grabbed the doorknob to his room, opened the door just enough, and closed it behind him. Then he ran to his bed, pulled back the layers of blankets, and climbed in, pulling the sheets over him before smashing his pillow into submission and laying his head down. The streetlamp was casting light from the window past the curtain and onto the floor. The wind howled outside as Tim turned away, facing the wall filled with sports and rock posters. The feeling of sleep came over him warm in his bed, drifting away somewhere in between sleep and dream as flickers of dark blue flashed behind his closed eyes until finally landing him fully into rest.

DREAMS OF THE ABYSS

Tim tossed and turned as he watched a blurry version of himself sitting on what looked to be a series of small logs tied together by frayed brown rope making for a loosely assembled raft. The water seemed colorless and almost like nothingness, more like the raft was floating on air with the occasional swirl or bubble appearing from somewhere below at random. The angle changed direction like a cut in a movie. Finally, Tim could no longer see himself but rather looked directly from his own eyes.

The dream went black for a moment almost as if to pause in darkness before resuming. Tim turned to see the sun rising in the sky and color beginning to form. The water turned blue; the raft looked different as the logs became planks and oars from side to side. Tim looked up and noticed he was up against a small mast leading to a bright white sail. It helped him glide along the calm, endless blue ocean.

Tim looked up beyond the sail to see white clouds gently floating against a soft blue background. Tim smiled and could feel almost guided to look over his shoulder at the rear of the raft. Tim turned his head, and with it, the raft now headed toward what seemed to be a coastline. The raft turned easy as Tim automatically knew just how to maneuver the oars, guiding direction with ease. Tim stood up and leaned against the mast with his head directly underneath the sail. He looked at the coast covered in white sand and trees overloaded with coconuts.

The trees dropped coconuts, but they disappeared before ever hitting the ground. So, Tim began to count the time until the next coconut would fall and go. The more they dropped, the better his timing until finally getting it right. He threw his hands up and laughed to signal victory.

Then the coast changed; the trees were gone and replaced with a smaller white beach beyond shallow water. The coral below sparkled with rocks peeking out over the blue, green gentle waves. Tim noticed Molly on a blanket with John lying beside her. Tim began to yell at the couple on the beach. They continued to laugh and smile, cuddling as the waves slowly began to rise and crash against the shoreline.

Then Tim turned his attention to a new feature behind the couple as a green jungle emerged in the distance. Tim watched it closely between the rise and fall of the waves as he continued to yell at the lovebirds. Finally, Dad emerged from the jungle, dragging a huge maul behind him through the white sand. He slowly made his way as the maul cut through the sand from the head's sheer weight. Tim began to wave his arms frantically and point as he yelled at his sister and John. Finally, Tim started to turn in his sleep, shifting from side to side as the wind continued to howl into the night.

The two began to kiss on the blanket as Tim grabbed the oars and tried to move closer, but, with every stroke, the rising waves pushed him back. Tim closed his eyes and thought of waking up as Dad reached John while Molly occupied him. Instead, Tim opened his eyes to complete silence, only to see Dad taking his first swing striking John in the head with the maul.

Molly moved from the blanket and began to scream and cry as maul and Dad smashed John's head into a mess of blood and pulp.

Tim fell to his knees and began to cry as well, watching his father destroy John. The jungle produced one more familiar person as Tim's mom appeared in her nurse outfit, sprinting across the sand toward the scene of blood-covered Molly, the blanket, and his dad as John was just an unrecognizable puddle of smashed flesh. His mom tried to scoop up the pieces as the bone and brains slipped through her wet gloves. She tried to put John back together while Molly cried, and Dad continued to crush him.

Tim finally let out one last scream. He continued to cry as he drifted in between the waves on the raft. His mom noticed his scream and stood up, calling his name, and waving her arms soaked in patchwork. Tim replied with renewed hope as the sun began to turn red, and the water blackened as night. Tim stopped as the shoreline and jungle disappeared with what was John and his family.

Tim knelt to see his reflection in the water. The waves stopped and drifted to a complete calm. The reflection rippled in the water as Tim stuck his hand in briefly, only to remove it. The water reflected and flowed red like the new sun and sky. It was blood red dripping from his fingers. Tim backed from the edge of the raft and sat back, placing his arm around the mast.

The feeling of turning his head came over him as he noticed a large black fin coming from the darkness. Tim stood up in a mad panic and grabbed the mast and tried closing his eyes. He could no longer see through them but looked on out of his own body like before. He saw the fin move closer as a giant set of teeth and large black eyes emerged from the water.

The raft was broken with one bite, throwing the mast and Tim into the air. He watched himself submerge and surface to hold onto the mast and scream as the fin circled for a while. Then, the black eye of the beast emerged again with the teeth and bit down on him. Tim could hear the crunch of his bones as he saw himself slowly consumed by the monster until there was nothing left of him, and the broken raft separated into the black.

"Tim," a voice called out as all went dark, followed by blue and blurry light. Tim shook as he threw off his covers and sat up in bed. His mom continued to call his name. The memory of the dream faded quickly from his mind as he replied to his mother's calls with a simple yes. He gathered his clothes for the day, pausing to look around the room and struggling to remember just what his dream was about and why his heart was still racing. Finally, Tim decided to pass off his vision and make his bed. He reached to grab some flannel pajama bottoms, placing them on one leg at a time and securing them around his waist.

The Saturday began as Tim took his clothes, opened his door, and ran down the hall to the bathroom to take on the day. A quick shower later, followed by a scramble to get dressed, Tim finally emerged as he ran down the hall and into his room. Tossing his pajamas on the bed before grabbing a cigarette pack from the stash and stuffing his sock, Tim grabbed his shoes from the corner of the room and slipped them on. He tied them tight before grabbing his sweatshirt and football, securing them under his arm and slamming the door on the way from his room. Tim skipped steps as he made it to the bottom of the stairs. He turned down the hall, which opened into the kitchen.

His mother sat perched on a stool still in her nurse's uniform. She smiled at Tim. She pointed at the spread of bacon, eggs, and pancakes stacked on the counter. His father sat across the table from Mom, sipping coffee and reading the morning paper. Looking over the article just enough, he cleared his throat. "Jane, ask your boy about the movie he watched last night." Tim looked at his mom and shrugged a bit. Then, adjusting his football, he began his prompted explanation of sharks eating people. His mom gasped and looked at her husband. "Thomas," she shrieked, "you know I don't like scary movies!" Thomas laid the paper on the table, laughing at her reaction.

    Tim seized the opportunity to leave after grabbing a handful of bacon from the plate on the counter. He asked where Molly was to shift his parents' focus. Jane looked up at Tim, who was standing between her and the breakfast. "This morning, Molly is over at the library discussing Homecoming with the girls," Jane mentioned, watching Tim devour the bacon. He placed his football next to breakfast plates before stuffing a few more bacon pieces in his mouth. Then, reaching for more, he paused as both parents watched his disregard for breakfast rules. Finally, his dad shifted focus from his staring contest with Tim and looked at the empty chairs. His mother cleared her throat and poured the juice into a glass from a porcelain pitcher, which sat slightly sweating. "Tim," his father said while Tim was still chewing up the bacon. "I can remember when I watched a scary movie for the first time." He broke into a story but was interrupted by Jane telling Tim to go while he has a chance.

    Thomas turned and looked at Jane before grabbing up the paper and continuing to read. "Next time, sit," Jane mentioned with firmness to her voice before cracking a bit of a smile. Jane turned her attention back to Thomas, who was reading the fine print of the sports page. She began to have a one-way conversation with him over the emergency room traffic last night. Tim looked back at his parents one last time and said, "I will be home for dinner." He opened the door to start his Saturday adventure with his sweatshirt tied around his waist and football in hand.

BALLS, BLOOD, AND RICKY CLARK

Tim observed all the Saturday morning activity around him as he made his way down the street toward the park. Tim let his imagination prepare him for today's football as he juked and stomped down the sidewalk, calling out plays and drawing cheers from the wind as if he were in a professional arena. Time and distance became a blur as the path taken became automatic and the escape from reality intense. The sideshow halted as Tim realized he had intersected the library, immediately placing himself in private spy mode.

There was no sign of Susie—only Molly in the parking lot, with her arms resting on the driver's side window of a truck with John seated inside. Tim passed by without being noticed and paused his steps. Images of John getting smashed by a hammer flickered behind his eyes like a movie frame. The efforts resumed as Tim forgot the picture. He felt relieved that his sister did not see him and ruin his football intention for the day.

Tim finally reached the tunnel that dead-ended the street and connected to the park. Then the flashbulbs flickered, and his name came blasting over the loudspeaker from the announcer. The cheers returned as Tim slowly walked through the tunnel, seeing the fans in his mind. The light at the end of the tunnel became narrowed as his mind raced with illusions of football glory. The flicker of magic stopped as the loudspeaker began to crack like bones breaking. The crowd started to cheer harder as the sky opened, raining blood. Tim, panicked by his visions, closed his eyes, and ran blindly through the rest of the tunnel. A familiar voice brought him back to reality as he opened his eyes. Tim noticed the outline of a person standing at the tunnel exit with the daylight behind him.

A voice called out, "Stove Top," and Tim's temporary anguish turned to delight, and he smiled. Tim shifted his football to his right. He placed his hand on the shoulder of the figure and returned a greeting of his own.

"Hey, Ricky. How are you?" Tim looked on, continuing to smile. Ricky brushed back the red hair covering his brow and smiled.

"Let's go; everyone is here and ready to play!" The two boys sprinted down the walking track. This led to the small field dotted by friends.

Tim rolled his football on the ground in a bowling motion as everyone began to gather. He untied his sweatshirt and placed it on a bench. Ricky called out to everyone, and the team selection began. The method was decided by a regular competition of Rock Paper Scissors. This led to Tim and Carl Mahone getting the team captain honors. The final match gave Tim the first pick. He landed Ricky as the teams were completed.

The new groups separated into huddles as Tim and his offense began to craft the first play. The offense lined up. Tim looked at the six defenders in front of him. Chris Matthews hiked the ball as Tim went into blocker mode, and the Mississippi count commenced. Tim backed up, looking downfield as Ricky raced away from the Fraley brothers. The eight-count passed, and Tim threw as hard as he could. The ball floated high in the sky and connected to Ricky's hands as Ricky ran down the field to score. Tim jumped with excitement as he could hear the crowd roaring in his mind once more.

Ricky trotted back to the huddle as the team switched to defense. Carl Mahone stood behind Justin Fraley as he began to hike the ball. Tim started to count as Carl gave Bobby Fraley the ball, who crossed behind him to run. Tim and Chris tackled Bobby before he gained a step, causing a fumble that Tim recovered before being tackled by Carl and Justin. Tim lined up again on offense for the next play and hiked the ball again. Tim was counting. Justin Fraley grabbed Tim, pushing him to the ground. "Eat shit," Fraley blurted as he looked down at Tim. Ricky charged full speed and tackled Justin, knocking him to the ground. Bobby, Chris, and then the rest of the kids soon joined in.

The pile-up left only Tim absent as he returned to his feet. Tim grabbed the football from the ground and went to retrieve his sweatshirt as the kids separated from the pile. Ricky and Justin exchanged words as Ricky wiped blood from his nostril. "Stove Top," Ricky called out as he watched Tim leaving. "I am done," Tim replied forcefully as he began to walk up the hill. "I don't like those Fraley boys," Tim grumbled as Ricky caught up to him.

"Where are you going now?" Ricky inquired as he looked back at the rest of the kids in the distance.

"I am going home," Tim whispered as his voice had a hint of depth in tone. Ricky ran past Tim and up the hill above the tunnel to the train tracks. "Stove Top, come with me," Ricky called out as he looked down at Tim, who paused while still looking at the ground. Tim finally looked up as Ricky continued to call on him. "Let's walk the tracks to my house and hang out," Ricky cheered while throwing his arms up in excitement. Tim looked at the tunnel and the path home. Tim nodded his head to Ricky as he ran up the hill to join him.

FERTILE DIRT STUDIO

The two friends began the journey out of town to the Clark Farm. "Finally, we can talk about Susie Meyer." Ricky giggled as he waited for a reaction from Tim. Tim stopped walking, looking around before reaching down into his sock for a pack of cigarettes and matches. "The coast is clear. We are out of town, and this is going to require a cigarette or two," Tim mumbled with laughter as he raised his eyebrow to almost attempt to remain sincere. Tim bent down to strike the first match against the rusty rails, lighting his cigarette. As he puffed, he lit a second from the first one. Ricky took the second cigarette from Tim and began smoking as the two boys continued the walk. "I like Susie," Tim said as he looked at Ricky for rebuttal. Ricky just continued to puff away and listen.

"I don't have time for her," Tim continued as the focus changed to Molly. "I have to help out my sister until she moves out."

"What does that mean?" Ricky asked.

"It means my sister is in love, and she is giving me cigarettes," Tim said as he slapped Ricky on the chest and smiled as he drew another drag. They looked at the fields before walking off the tracks and down the gravel road leading to the farm.

Walking to the porch, they entered the house through the kitchen. Sitting at the table was Ricky's mother, June, who smiled and asked the boys if they were hungry. The boys looked at two freshly baked apple pies sitting in front of her. June got up from the table and went to the refrigerator, pulling out the ham, cheese, and mayonnaise. "Let me fix you a sandwich and get you some milk; you can have the pie for dessert." The boys sat at the table as June made them both plates and milk glasses before sitting to talk to them.

"You know, boys, the harvest will be here soon and then Halloween. Of course, Halloween was always my favorite," she said as she smiled at the boys.

Ricky spoke up and said, "Mom, we are too old for trick or treat."

June looked at Ricky and said, "It is more than that; it's about the end of a season and another year for the spirits to have one night to walk the earth again. See, Ricky, there are many things we just do not understand, do we? Now, finish up your sandwiches, and I'll let you take your pie out and enjoy it under the maple."

The boys finished up and took their plates and slices of apple pie to the old maple tree, where they sat by the trunk eating as they watched the falling leaves. When they finished, they took the plates back inside and placed them in the sink as June rested in her rocker. They ran out the door and into the field. Tim ran as fast as he could between the rows of corn. He came to a complete stop as he noticed something lying directly in his path. Ricky, unable to stop in time, crashed into Tim, knocking them both to the ground. Tim was first to his feet as he pointed and said, "Ricky Look at that!" The two boys walked further up the rise and stopped with a carcass at their feet.

"It's a deer," Ricky said as he studied carefully. Claw marks covered the dead animal, and prints covered the soil.

"What could have done this?" Tim asked as he learned Ricky's detective skill.

Ricky turned and looked at Tim as he kicked the carcass, disturbing the flies, and hollered, "Cayotee! Now run, Stove Top!" The boys laughed as they ran back to wash up by the windmill and the water pump before lying down underneath the maple tree beside the barn.

The two boys drifted off to sleep as the breeze blew over them. The drift of time became present as the morning swelled into the afternoon. The boys slumbered until the sun was well past noon and evening was approaching. The boys were awakened by the sound of a horn as Mr. Clark pulled the farm truck into the drive. It sputtered and banged. Tim and Ricky got up and shook off the grass and sleepiness as Mr. Clark parked his truck and got out to greet the boys. "Tim, how are ya, kid?" Mr. Clark asked.

"Fine, sir," Tim replied as he brushed the leaves off his sweatshirt.

"You boys having a good day?" Mr. Clark questioned.

Both boys nodded and said, "Yes, sir."

"I got this old truck fixed up today," Mr. Clark declared. "All ready for harvest coming up." Mr. Clark looked out over the field around the farm. "Tim, do you need a ride home?" urged Mr. Clark.

Tim said, "I will be fine, but I really should be going; I don't want Dad to get mad." Mr. Clark smiled as Tim waved goodbye. He grabbed his football and ran toward the road. As he neared the tracks, Tim began to think about Susie, then his sister and the help he has given her. But Tim continued to weigh his feelings as the rails led the way into town. Finally, Tim decided to walk past the park and onto Susie's street in hopes of seeing her. As he turned the corner onto her street, he crossed the path of Justin and Bobby Fraley. Before he could turn and go the other way, the brothers spotted him. They began to chase Tim as his already-tired self tried to run several blocks to his house.

Tim crossed the field where he played football earlier and made his way back to the tunnel. He paused to catch his breath and looked behind him before walking into the tunnel. Steady and clutching the football under his arm, Tim continued to proceed down the old tunnel. Before he reached the end, he got hit from behind.

Tim was knocked to the ground and kicked by both brothers. Tim tried to catch his breath as the brothers stopped kicking; he slid up the wall to get to his feet. Justin grabbed Tim by the throat and said, "This is for you and your faggot friend Ricky!" Justin punched Tim in the face, forcing him to collapse to the ground. He laid on the ground and began to cry as the brothers took his football and ran down the tunnel. Then, finally, the two brothers disappeared into the fast-approaching evening.

Calming enough to catch his breath, Tim felt his face where he was punched as the swelling started. Tim returned to his feet, leaning against the wall to make his way out of the tunnel. Stepping into the light, Tim looked at the dirt on his clothes and arms and grabbed his side where he was kicked. Tim moved down the sidewalk, shuffling his feet along as he continued to progress.

The walk seemed the most prolonged all day, and the frequent stops made it seem further from home. Tim finally crossed the street to his home as the sun began to fade. Tim looked up to see Molly sitting on the porch swing and made his way to the steps. Molly looked at Tim and hurried off the swing to help him up the steps. Tim sat on the swing, relieved to be finally home. Molly went inside to get their parents. Thomas arrived shortly as he knelt and placed his hand on Tim's shoulder.

"Tell me, son, what happened?" Tim recalled how he played football and went to Ricky's house before being jumped by the brothers in the park tunnel when he was returning home. Thomas stood up, grabbed the keys from his pocket. "I will show you how I deal with thugs!" Thomas helped Tim to the truck as Molly then Jane emerged from the house. "I will be back in a bit," Thomas hollered as he got in the driver's seat and backed the truck from the drive. Thomas asked Tim, "Where do these boys live?" Tim replied as he groaned in pain, "At the dead end of Patterson Hill by the river."

Thomas stepped on the gas as the truck hopped over the rise. Thomas asked Tim how he felt as they arrived at the hill's bottom and the entrance to a lane. Tim countered, "I will be OK, just sore from all of the walking."

Thomas placed the truck in park and said, "I need you to walk just a bit more. When we are done, you are going to the hospital." Thomas got out, grabbing the tire iron from behind the seat to walk around to the passenger side and help Tim out of the truck.

They both walked down the lane. They passed trash and old junk cars before they arrived at an old, broken-down shack with water in the yard mixed with trash and piles of old screen doors. Thomas hollered to the hut as the shadows moved around the dim light inside. "Fraley, get out here, or I will burn you out, and no one will care!" The two boys exited the shack, followed by their father. Claude Fraley was as round as he was tall with a pair of tattered bibs covering his massive frame. Fraley stepped in front of them off the porch.

"For what?" Claude responded sternly as he crossed his arms.

Thomas stepped up to Claude as he replied, "Your fuckin boys ganged up on my boy and beat him for no reason!"

Claude looked at his boys and said, "Is this true?"

Thomas waited and became angrier. Justin spoke up first and said "yes" followed by Bobby. Then Justin spoke again and said, "That is only because he is a faggot and winked at us at the park."

Tim looked at the boys and said, "That is a lie; you boys got mad because you were losing!"

Claude looked at Tim and said, "My boys aren't losers, and maybe they tell the truth. You look like a weak faggot!"

Thomas lowered his brow, and his voice deepened as he spoke. "I spent years in a war to come home and raise my son to be tough. He is not what you say, and any action against him is against me!" Claude prepared to speak again, but before the words could flow, Thomas grabbed him by the throat and said, "I will show you hell!" He began to strike Claude down with the tire iron. Thomas's anger turned to straight rage as Claude fell to the ground, and the beating continued. Then, lastly, Thomas hollered at the Fraley boys, "All you had to do is leave my boy alone; instead, you insult him and mock me!"

The boys began to cry as Thomas continued to strike. "Please stop," Bobby Fraley cried. Justin got down on his knees. Tim looked on at what his father had done, and it reminded him why he covered for his sister. Tim began to cry and asked his dad to please stop. Thomas let go of Claude, who was bruised and bleeding but still conscious.

"If you boys lay one finger on my son or his friends ever again, I will personally come back and kill you all. Now help your dad back into that shit hole you call home." Tim and his father walked back up the lane and to the truck. "Tim, get in the truck now; we are leaving!"

Tim responded directly to his father's command and got in the truck. Thomas threw the bloody tire iron in the bed and wiped his hand off in the grass before getting in the driver's seat. "Dad, is he going to die?" Tim asked between the pain and trying not to cry.

Thomas looked at Tim and said, "I broke his nose and bruised his face; he will feel that for a while, but he will live. Tim, you and your sister and Mom are all that matter to me. I am to protect you, and I take that very seriously!"

Tim rested his head against the truck door as they drove off into the night. Tim listened to the rumble of the truck as he pondered with his eyes closed. Then, finally, the bright lights of the hospital caused him to sit up.

Thomas parked outside the emergency room as he shut the truck off and went around to help Tim. Tim shuffled across the parking lot with his father into the hospital. Nurse Rhodes waited at reception got up to help Tim into a room before getting the doctor. The emergency room was quiet as Tim sat on the bed, and Thomas looked around the quiet hallway. Dr. Brady emerged from an office and made his way to the room.

"Hello, I am Dr. Brady," he said as he shook the firm hand of Thomas. Tim sat up as Dr. Brady began to ask questions. "Tell me what happened?" Dr. Brady asked as he checked Tim's pulse.

"I was walking home and got beat up by two boys."

Dr. Brady responded, "Show me where you are hurting." Tim pulled up his shirt, revealing several bruises on his chest. The doctor gently touched the bruises as he listened with a stethoscope, instructing Tim to breathe in and out. Finally, the doctor finished his exam and offered his opinion as he stood writing on a clipboard.

The doctor said, "Nothing is broken, but there is some bruising, and you are going to have to take it easy for a few weeks. Ice will go a long way in helping you feel better and reduce some of the inflammation." Thomas thanked the doctor as he got ready to get the nurse for discharge, Tim asked, "Do you know my mom?" The doctor hesitated as Tim said, "Jane Stover."

Thomas smiled at the doctor as he said, "I did not even make the connection."

"I bet your mom is worried about you," Thomas said as he looked at Tim and the doctor. "She is home waiting and should help in the recovery."

"Fantastic," said the doctor as he left the room. The doctor passed the nurse the chart as he returned to his office. The nurse arrived to repeat the information. Thomas thanked the nurse, helping Tim down the hall to the exit.

The two of them got back in the truck and began the trip home. The trip seemed noticeably short. As the truck pulled into the driveway and they exited the truck, Thomas looked at Tim and said, "All we did was go to the hospital and nothing more." Thomas said, "Keep everything else that happened just between us." Tim nodded out of fear and respect as they walked up to the porch and into the house. Tim slowly entered the house behind his father and made his way up the stairs to wash up for dinner. Jane let Tim pass and stopped Thomas at the entrance to the kitchen.

Jane asked, "Is Tim all right?"

Thomas placed his hand on Jane's shoulder as he looked at her and Molly before replying, "Yes, Tim is sore, but it will be fine. The Fraley boys beat him bad when he was walking back from Clark Farm. Let us all sit down and eat; it has been a long day."

Thomas entered the dining room as Jane and Molly moved aside, finding his seat at the table's head. Molly and Jane followed and sat, waiting for Tim to arrive. Tim made his way slowly to the dining room, seating himself at an already full dining room table. Tim looked at Molly as dinner was passed around the table. "Hey, sis, did you find anything useful at the library?"

Molly smiled and said, "The typical light reading." Tim cut into his porkchop and took a bite.

Jane looked at him and said, "I know you are fifteen, but these late walks to Clark's need to stop for a while. All of the problems this evening and my long hours this week followed by your father's work and overtime—do you understand my concern?"

Tim nodded, and Dad went back to eating after realizing Tim would keep what happened away from Mom. As everyone talked, Tim continued to be engrossed in eating and thinking about a cigarette. After dinner, Molly and Jane cleaned the dining room and finished the dishes. Thomas disappeared into the den to watch TV and nap.

Tim took the trash out to the curb. Tim looked down the quiet street as he pulled the last cigarette out of his sock. He lit a smoke sitting on the curb, concealing himself from the house. Tim reflected on his day, and a flicker of his dream surfaced— just those black, lifeless eyes and the sound of bones breaking. Tim finished his cigarette and went back into the house. As he headed up to his room, Molly called for Tim. As he stood in the doorway, she whispered with a smile, "How are the cigarettes?"

Tim smiled. "How is John?"

"Are we on for Friday?" Molly asked. Tim nodded as he headed back to his room.

Tim finished his nightly ritual, turned out the lights, and settled into bed, hoping for a night without dreams as his mind faded from reality. Instead, the morning came early as Tim was awakened by the smell of bacon in the air. He stumbled out of bed, threw on a pair of shorts, and followed the scent into the kitchen. Relieved he had no dream, Tim said good morning to his mother, who was busy cooking away. Molly and his father sat in the dining room, sharing coffee and a conversation about Richard Nixon. "Tim, go up and get a shower before you eat, so we are ready for church on time." Without responding, Tim made his way upstairs, gathered his clothes, and made his way into the shower.

Tim appeared at the table a short time later, joining everyone for breakfast. Everyone laughed and was at peace with one another, and Sunday mornings seemed to bring closure to the week, and everything became new again in the Stover house. Now, church disagreed with Tim, and he felt the best part of his day had passed when he left the breakfast table and headed to the car. But Jane was all about church, and every Sunday was her idea. The minute everyone got in the station wagon and left the street, Jane began her church sermon from the passenger seat as everyone sat silent. She repeated the same topics for twenty minutes as the car headed away from Riverside to Maple Grove, where she grew up.

The village housed a few churches, but it was the little brick church downtown that Jane grew up in. As the wagon pulled into the stone lot beside the church, Tim and Molly quickly exited the car because they knew at least in church that they did not have to pay attention if they sat in the back. They were drained after Mother's traveling sermon and too late for Sunday school.

THE WAGES OF SIN

Tim sat next to his sister in the rows of pews, placing them in the center of the church. He was lost in thought as he pretended to listen and recount in the group. The preacher hooked Tim when he brought forth one phrase—payment for the wages of sin. The cost of crime was more than just the admission of guilt and cleansed forgiveness. It was a battle for the soul doing what we know is wrong and allowing ourselves to continue—the invitation to evil and the prospect that we were opening the door to whatever lies on the other side.

As the preacher spoke, Tim reflected on his own actions; he was hooked for sure. Was this his invitation to evil, trading lies for cigarettes? Was his sister in sin? What will she invite in her life as a result? Worried for a moment, Tim smiled and remembered this was the preacher's role in provoking these thoughts, and this notion of sin was a measure of perfection. Everybody sins; everyone in this church has lied, cheated, or stolen, and it was this hook, this foreboding guilt, that kept them all stirring. Tim looked at his parents; what sin have they committed? They seem to be strangers to his ideal. He had not known them to invite evil in. Why were they here? Was it for them or for us? If so, what do they know? If they have been preparing us in this small-town church to wage war against sin by endless conversation, then they have failed. Tim looked at his sister as she doodled squiggle lines on her pamphlet tucked underneath her hymn book. *Should I be helping her sneak around?* Tim thought, *What will be the outcome when Mom and Dad are finally aware of what she is doing and what I know about it? How will this affect what they believe we are, what our family is, and what this day means?*

    Tim shook his head and turned to his hymn book for the final song refresher. When service concluded, Tim was the first out to the car and rolled down the window. Between the fresh fall air and lack of conversation, at times Tim napped on the way home. Once home, Tim disappeared into his room without so much as a conversation with anyone. Honestly bothered by the day and the weeks of sneaking, Tim centered his activities at his study desk and finished his Friday homework. He sought to figure out a way to remove himself from the lies and sneaking without damaging his relationship with his sister.

    As the day faded and turned into evening, Tim headed downstairs to see his mother off to work. She stood at the door saying goodbye to Thomas and Molly dressed in her nurse's outfit with her pointy bonnet placed on her head. "Off to work," Jane said. Tim hugged her side while Jane turned to walk out the front door. Tim watched her fade into the car as the lights blinked on, and she drove off. Tim went off to the kitchen, searched the fridge for cold leftovers from yesterday's meal, and went to the table to eat alone.

    Tim placed his plate in the sink and sought out his father, who was sleeping in the den. Tim told him good night and urged him to make it to bed as well. Thomas cracked a smile and turned over on the old leather couch to indicate he was already committed to it for the night. Tim searched for his sister but found her already asleep in her room. Tim went to his room down the hall. He finished his night and settled into rest. He made a point to erase his thoughts and empty his mind to sleep easily.

FERTILE DIRT STUDIO

―

The shift started off as a quiet night in the emergency room. Jane walked up the inclined hallway to the nurse's lounge. Underneath the flickering fluorescent, she sat reading over a copy of the morning's newspaper that had been left behind and picked apart. As she read on and flipped around for something of interest, Dr. Brady entered the lounge. Standing by the coffee pot, he proceeded to turn and smile at Jane. He poured himself a cup of black and walked down the hall, vanishing into the supply room. Jane placed the paper down in pursuit of something more interesting and walked into the supply room where she found Dr. Brady leaning up against a shelf of supplies, sipping his coffee. Jane shut the door and locked it and proceeded to walk toward the doctor. The doctor asked how Tim was doing, and Jane responded, "Fine." The doctor told her he had a seminar in Toledo and wanted to know if she could get away. Jane agreed to try as she undid her blouse and reached for the doctor's zipper. She undid his zipper, lowered her head, and began to work on the doctor. Moments later, they both emerged from the storage room, fixed up as though nothing had happened.

"Thanks for your help, Dr. Brady," Jane said as she loaded the cart's contents from the storage room. The doctor replied, "Anytime," as he walked down the hall into his office. Jane carted supplies down the hall to the emergency room to find Mrs. Jones at registration, doing her crosswords at the desk.

"Anything tonight, Mrs. Jones?" Jane asked as she put supplies away.

"Nope, we had a report across the scanner of a car wreck earlier out on ninety-two. The deputy thinks an animal crossed the road. The driver ran off into a cornfield to avoid it. No injuries to report. They have not found the driver yet. Deputy Mills thinks the driver may either be drunk or have wandered off to find the animal. There is blood on the bumper; something got hit."

Jane looked at Mrs. Jones and said, "That's out there where Mr. Clark lives down by the drive-in; my boy was just out there Saturday, but he walks the tracks back into town."

Mrs. Jones replied, "It's getting close to harvest time. Animals are getting restless." Jane shrugged as she made her way down the hall to check on her patients. She walked into room 108 to find Mrs. Mercer sitting up reading a book.

"How are you, Jane?" Mrs. Mercer smiled, looking over her book.

Jane said, "Excellent, just a quiet night," as she went to check vitals. "We had a wreck on ninety-two; the deputy is still investigating." Mrs. Mercer sat up a bit to get comfortable and folded her book in her lap.

"You know my nephew Allen came to live with me at the farm years ago. His mind was different. After my husband, George, passed away. Allen returned from the war and took up the farming. In the spring and summer, Allen worked the land and kept busy day and night. In the fall, when the corn was tall and harvest time was near, Allen changed, and it got worse over the years. He used to sit in the swing and stare at the field and watch the corn blow in the breeze. The years went by; he would take the old Winchester off the wall and walk into the areas patrolling. He said they were out there; he could hear them. That the harvest is here." Mrs. Mercer grabbed Jane by the wrist with her old, wrinkled hand. She looked at Jane with her sunken gray eyes. "He disappeared and left in the field and never came back. Sheriff Davis looked all over the farm and the lands and found nothing." Mrs. Mercer let go and said, "Maybe he was just restless and moved on after that damn war." Jane shivered a bit and left the room with vitals completed. Mrs. Mercer picked up her book and continued reading as if to forget the incident.

Jane walked back down the hall, looked at Mrs. Jones, and asked for any word from that wreck. "Yes, Deputy Mills said over the scanner that Jack Harlowe, the driver, went looking for the animal he hit and could not tell what it was. He wandered into the field and could not find his way back. The deputy finally called him out. Harvest!" Mrs. Jones said as she looked at Jane. Jane, steadied by the update, wondered in her mind about Mrs. Mercer and her nephew. Was it dementia? Why couldn't she remember her nephew? Did he really disappear? Was he even there? Maybe her sense of time was off, and he left before the war and did not come back. Lost in thought, Jane bumped into Dr. Brady as she went around the corner. Dr. Brady smiled and said, "I wasn't too rough on you, was I?" Before Jane could reply, the double doors opened, and two EMTs appeared pushing a gurney with a man screaming in pain and covered in blood. The doctor quickly directed them to a room as he told Jane to get supplies. The doctor asked the men what happened, and before they could answer, Deputy Walton entered the room.

"I shot this man on accident. I was investigating a report of trespassers at my cousin Billy's farm when Bob Arkin startled me around the backside of the barn. He came up behind me. I shot and got him in the shoulder." Jane brought the scissors, and she began to cut the blood-soaked clothes off Bob's chest. The EMTs strapped Bob in as Jane numbed the wound with a needle. She kept pressure with a compress. Dr. Brady removed the compress and worked to dig out the bullet with grips. Once removed, he sewed up the injury.

Bob calmed down, apologized to the deputy, and said he was a hired hand for the Walton's for harvest. "There has been some strange activity up on the ridge behind the farm. We had a goat and a pig come up missing, and there is a path leading through the field beyond the old orchard up on the hill. I was on my way back when I saw you behind the barn and just wanted to tell you what I saw."

"What did you see?" asked the deputy.

"Hell," Bob said, "They were on the hill, fire blazing, dancing naked, and chanting. They brought the goat, the one that looked like the leader. He did the unspeakable to that animal before they cut its throat and smeared the blood all over their flesh. They started on each other in a pile of blood and sex. Then the leader came back with the pig and fed it the goat's flesh before cutting off its head and dancing around a pile of people, holding the pig's head and chanting as they lusted over each other. I thought they saw me. I ran like heck down the hill and saw you." With that, Bob passed out from the trauma.

Jane walked out of the room and began to cry as she scrubbed the blood off her. She was terrified as images filled her head. Tim had been walking the tracks north of town for months and is lucky he was not harmed. As she dried her hands and tears, she walked from the washroom; she overheard the deputy tell Dr. Brady this was not the first time, and they have been investigating this for years. "It's all Satan worship," the deputy said. "We believe it is widespread in this area due to the old history." The doctor shook his head as he turned to notice Jane and said to her, "Nurse Williams is coming down from B wing; why don't you go home? Get some rest; this has been a traumatic event for all of us. I will walk you out to the car."

Not resistant, Jane walked out through the lobby with the doctor and to her wagon. She got in, thanked the doctor, and drove off as he stood in the lot watching her leave. As Jane drove down the empty city street, the stillness of the night calmed her. She just wanted to get to the refuge of her home and let the current events drift away. Before she realized it, she was sitting at her drive in front of the house. Lost in thought, the journey was automatic. Finally, Jane turned the car off and walked into the house.

She immediately made her way to the den to find Thomas passed out on the old leather couch. She watched him for a moment as he slumbered and then gently shook him to gain his attention. "Thomas," she spoke as she proceeded to nudge.

Thomas peeked with one eye and then replied as he sat up, "Janie, what's wrong? Are you OK? The kids!" Thomas mumbled as he opened both eyes.

"Tom, it was horrible! A man was shot, and the d-devil," Jane stuttered as she began to sob.

Thomas said, "What devil? Who shot? Huh?" He put his hand on her shoulder and told her to calm down.

Jane began "The Walton Farm, again off ninety-two; a farm hand was shot by David Walton while investigating a trespass; oh, it was an accident." Jane sobbed, "A horrible accident." Jane looked at Thomas as she brushed the hair off her wet cheek. "The man is all right, but what he said, Thomas, oh God, it was horrible."

Thomas said, "What?"

Jane said, "Devil worship on the hill behind the farm, blood, animals missing, and sex on the sacrifice."

Thomas looked Jane in the eyes and said, "It's OK; the sheriff will take care of it."

Jane replied, "You don't understand! Tim walks to the Clark Farm out there; he has already been hurt, but it could be worse, and we let him do it; who are we?"

Thomas said, "OK, we will stop all drive-in and long walks until the sheriff gets this under control." Jane calmed as Thomas rubbed the back of her neck and nodded in agreement with the proposed solution.

Thomas proceeded to kiss Jane as he smiled and said, "You are home early." Thomas stood up removing his clothes. Next, Thomas slid his hands down on Jane's breast, removing one from her dress. Kissing her nipple as he proceeded to maneuver her on the couch, where he pulled her panties and lay her open at the legs to drive his cock deep into her. Jane closed her eyes and tried to enjoy his thrust, but all she could think about was Dr. Brady. Then without reason, the images in her mind shifted to the fire burning in the night. The bodies of people covering each other in blood and fucking in piles made her mind drift. She began to get excited as Thomas thrust harder; she could feel the heat from the flames as Thomas pulled at her buttons, exposing both breasts. Finally, she imagined herself in a pile with the doctor and her husband as they smeared blood and sex all over each other.

She could feel herself cum as Thomas pushed deeper with her legs on his shoulders. Thomas moaned as he thrust as her orgasm made it smoother, her nipples hard and body quivering. Finally, she pushed her hands against Thomas's chest and said, "Turn me over." Thomas backed up as Jane threw herself over the arm of the couch, lifting her skirt. Thomas found his way back in, pushing harder with her on her knees; the images in her head flickered faster between the fire and the two men sharing her. She peaked again as she bit into her wrist to muffle the moan. "My ass!" she shrieked in ecstasy, "Fuck my ass!" Thomas slid his cock into her hole as he spread her skinny white cheeks apart; his hard cock, ready to explode, he thrust as deep as his shaft would allow. The pain only amplified the images in her mind as the stranger moved into the pile; his cock was massive and throbbing in her mouth as the other participants worked her from all angles.

She felt her eyes roll back as her excitement ran down her leg. Then, with a final thrust, Thomas let loose his nut, filling her up as he backed out. Thomas sat back on his knees as Jane collapsed in pleasure on the couch with the hot cum oozing. Her mind cleared of the images. Then the guilt of her ecstasy arrived. Jane quickly got up, gathered her panties, bloused her breasts, and went down the hall to the bathroom to clean up. Thomas placed his pants back on and cleaned the couch stains with his shirt before heading down the entrance to the bathroom to join her.

The shower steamed hot as he removed his clothes, added them to the basket in the corner, and slid the glass door to climb in. Jane was under the head, letting the water flow over her naked body, as Thomas slid behind her, pressing his body against her. Thomas asked Jane if she was OK, and Jane replied, "Yes, just tired," as she moved away and proceeded to wash up. Thomas grabbed a cloth and began to lather himself and scrub as he said, "I will talk with the kids after school about the drive-in and the Clark Farm." Jane shook her head in agreement as she stepped out of the shower and grabbed a towel to dry off. Thomas stared at the drain as his mind wandered over what Jane had described earlier.

Finally, Thomas turned off the water, stepped out of the shower, dried himself off, and grabbed his robe off the back of the bathroom door. Thomas headed down the hall to finish a conversation with Jane as he entered the bedroom but found her already asleep. He sighed and removed his robe, climbing under the blankets beside her. As Thomas turned out the light, Jane opened her eyes and laid there silent, staring into the darkness.

THE PIG MASK

Thomas found himself in Vietnam with his old unit. The tangled jungle had been replaced with rows of corn. As his group moved through the rows, Thomas could feel someone watching. He locked the bolt on his rifle. He could see shadows moving in the rows ahead. Finally, a chopper moved overhead; the explosions started. His unit members were being blown to pieces, and the corn started to pop with every explosion. The popcorn was stained red as the field became flooded with it, and soldiers were dying as they were getting swallowed up in it. The level rose to his neck. Thomas felt unable to move, screaming for help; a shadow came from the distance and approached. It was a man with a pig's head and sharp teeth; it opened its full mouth and proceeded to bite Thomas's head. Thomas woke up to an empty bed and the morning sun poking through the blinds. He gathered his robe as the dream memory quickly faded, and he made his way to the kitchen.

    The sun rose into the gray sky and floated above the clouds as Davis, Walton, and Mills made their way up the hill past the orchard behind the Walton Farm. Smoke came from the bare ash-covered earth as they approached. Davis asserted, "Why the fuck didn't you two shit birds investigate this as it happened last night?"

    Mills shook his head as he looked at Walton and said, "I was investigating an accident, and Walton here was on the property."

Walton looked at Mills and said, "I shot someone last night, and you'll be next, dickhead." With that, Sheriff Davis stopped the two deputies and said, "All right, boys, gather evidence, and don't screw this up!"

The men circled the fire pit and kicked up the ash to look for details of the night's events. A murder of crows flew from the base of an old willow, directing the men toward the tree; there they found a pile of bones and burned pig remains with bloody handprints plastered on the trunk and the word *Satanas* carved into the wood. Walton looked at the sheriff and said, "Maybe we should call some investigators from Toledo on this one."

Davis said, "Let us rope this area off and get out of here; you boys get done, go home, and get some rest. I will call the Wood County office today. Tonight, you will patrol this area, and boys, keep your fuckin' eyes open." The two deputies and the sheriff made it to their vehicles, and the deputies drove away. Sheriff Davis called dispatch for any messages before leaving the scene. The dispatcher came back with a call from the hospital and said, "They have received a severely bruised up and disoriented patient. The ambulance brought him in and said they know the guy who did it; his boys are witnesses." The sheriff looked at the deputy's car as it pulled away and radioed to them to continue home for the day. "I will personally handle the investigation at the hospital."

Jane walked at the mall, looking for new work clothes to supplement her blood-stained nurse attire from the previous night. Looking at her reflection in the storefronts as she passed by the stores, she paused to notice a pig mask. Stopping to walk inside, Jane walked up behind the pig mask on display and stared down at it for a bit. Then, Jane began rubbing the top of the hood and the snout with her fingers as she closed her eyes momentarily and recounted the images.

She could feel her excitement with every finger stroke and began to feel wet when a hand touched her shoulder and startled her. "Are you OK?" asked the clerk as she took a breath and turned to look at him. The clerk smiled as Jane looked up at him, and he tried not to notice her breasts visible through the low-cut blouse. "Did you like the mask?" which was now laying off the display shelf and on the floor.

Jane turned and picked the mask up, handed it to the clerk, and replied, "Yes, can you wrap this in a box for me? It's a gift for a friend."

The clerk wrote an address on a piece of paper and said, "Come to this address later, and you can have this mask." Jane looked at the clerk and nodded in agreement. The clerk looked on and smiled as Jane left the store.

"I will see you later," she said as she exited the open store entrance into the street. The clerk turned the mask with his hand inside face to face; he began to snort like a pig and laugh, then placed it in a box.

—

Thomas sat at the table, eating his usual self-cooked bacon and eggs. Thomas glanced at the counter from the table and fixed his eyes on the popcorn popper. He began thinking about his dream and blamed it on Vietnam in his mind. Thomas closed his eyes and could still feel the jungle around him and see the enemy's shadows moving around his unit before they attacked.

He could still smell the burnt powder and gun oil as he fired into the dark. He remembered the jungle burning around him as jets dropped napalm death. He remembered walking from the carnage alone as the chopper came down to pick him up.

Thomas opened his eyes, carried his cold breakfast to the sink, and finished his coffee. Then he walked down the hall to get ready for work only to reappear outside, reaching into his truck twenty minutes later. He read a note from Jane: *Tom, I ran to get new uniforms for work, doctors, and nurses convention this weekend in Toledo; we will talk about it tonight, Janie.* Thomas shook his head as he crumbled up the note and started the truck. Then, turning up the music on his favorite AM station, Thomas crossed town to the weld shop. He arrived at the time clock to punch in. Floyd Martin approached him. "Thomas," Floyd said, "I have Sheriff Davis in my office, and he would like to speak with you."

Thomas, stone-faced, followed Floyd through the plant to the back office by the series of docks. He noticed the sheriff's car parked outside through the open overhead door. Floyd entered the small office, followed by Thomas, and Floyd pointed to his desk opposite the sheriff. Thomas turned and looked at Floyd, who remained standing between him and the door as it closed.

"Good morning," the sheriff said as he raised his head and looked right at Thomas. "I don't believe we met before. I am Sheriff Michael Davis." Thomas interrupted and said, "Yeah, I have seen your campaign posters in the past, and I really don't care; what do you want with me?"

The sheriff turned his head, looked at Floyd, and remarked, "Wow, we have a real hard-ass here." The sheriff looked back at Thomas and said, "Well, that makes sense!" Thomas lowered his brow as the sheriff spoke again. "I just visited some of your alleged handywork at the emergency room. Fraley and his two boys said you worked him over well. I would like you to come with me over to my office until we get this figured out."

Thomas asked, "Am I under arrest?"

The sheriff replied, "Not yet, but you may want to get your attorney in mind in case I change my mind."

Thomas realized the weight of the situation and complied while thoughts of overpowering the sheriff and making a run for it crossed his mind. Thomas stood up as Floyd opened the door to the office, and he followed the sheriff and Floyd outside and down the stairs to where the sheriff's car was parked. Thomas paused and looked at both men and said again, "Does this mean...?"

The sheriff smiled as Thomas lowered his brow, and Floyd took two steps back. Then the sheriff said, "I just want to get you to the station and talk. That is all, but to be fair—because I really do not have all the facts yet—I did say an attorney may be necessary."

Thomas paused again and said, "What about my truck?"

The sheriff looked at Floyd and announced, "I am sure Floyd doesn't mind if we leave it here for a bit, do you, Floyd?"

Floyd said, "Not at all," as he shrugged at both men.

The sheriff said, "Mr. Stover, I will even let you ride up front; how about that?" Thomas stepped forward and opened the passenger door before looking around the lot one more time and getting in the vehicle. The sheriff sat in the driver's seat and said, "Thank you for cooperating, Thomas, that means a lot to me." Floyd watched from the lot before turning to walk back. The two men left in the squad car as Thomas watched Floyd in the passenger mirror.

Tim and Ricky were sitting outside after lunch before the next class discussing football when Susie walked up. "Hi, Tim," she said as she turned to ignore Ricky and his series of faces. Tim stood up and said hi to Susie. "Tim are you going to the drive-in?" she asked as she smiled.

Tim said, "If you are going to be there already, don't count on seeing me, but I will have to ask my sister if possible." Susie smiled and replied, "OK then." She turned her head and walked over to her friends.

Ricky looked at Tim and shook his head, "Man, your sister will never go for that."

Tim grumbled as he replied, "I know." Tim was troubled. He watched as the schoolyard emptied back into the building and followed from behind. The sky was still gray and fluid, hiding the sun.

Sheriff Davis and Thomas arrived at the sheriff's department. Thomas sighed as he got out of the car and was led in the back door of the sheriff's brick building. The sheriff and Thomas walked down a short hallway that led into an open room. Thomas looked down the hall and noticed the dispatch desk and four cells with thick bars on three sides, beds, and a toilet. Thomas took a seat as the sheriff joined him at the opposite side of the office.

The sheriff sat down and smiled at Thomas before speaking. "Thomas, I appreciate honesty, and it will go a long way with me. Now, before we get started, you need to understand this. You are not free to go at any time. I will be glad to take you back to your vehicle, but until I am satisfied in this matter, we are not done with you."

Thomas looked directly at the sheriff and questioned, "What is the other option?"

The sheriff smiled again and said, "You cooperate, and all of this becomes nice and easy." Thomas nodded as the sheriff said,

"Excellent, let's continue. I have here three statements that tell the other night you and your son arrived at the Fraley residence somewhere around six thirty, and an altercation ensued between you and Claude Fraley. This altercation resulted in you beating Mr. Fraley with a tire iron to the point where his face looks like a purple puffball, and he suffers from cuts, a broken nose, and a concussion. That is some real serious shit you just stepped into, the point of being a felony, and given whatever prior history with violence you may or may not have, maybe probation or prison." The sheriff looked at Thomas and said, "Why the hell did you have to use an iron? You seem like a big man I would not want to square off with, and Claude looks like a pile of mushy potatoes, all lumpy covered in bibs." The sheriff said, "Well, go on. I want you to tell me what happened and help me understand. Now, remember, as a caution, make me a believer because if you do, this gets a lot easier."

Thomas sat back in his chair and looked around the room before speaking. "I am not a lawbreaker, and I do believe in right and wrong. I have only been home for a little over two years now and spent several years before that in Nam."

The sheriff looked intrigued as he reached for his pipe on the desk, dumping the ash into the trash, filling it with new tobacco, and lighting it. "Continue," the sheriff said as he smoked his pipe, and tobacco smell filled the office.

Thomas proceeded to address the sheriff through the plume of smoke. "I returned home, and all I have wanted is to resume my life like before the war and care for and protect my family."

The sheriff asked, "Well, you are in your middle thirties and probably didn't get drafted, so how did you end up going over there?"

"My younger brother served and enlisted when the war started when he was twenty, and I already had a family. Molly and Tim were both tiny, but my brother and I were awfully close. My father was a drunk, and my mother had left when we were young, so all Tim and I had was each other. I was worried that he would not come back so, I decided to enlist with him, and I was right."

"So, your brother and your son are both named Tim. What happened to your brother?"

"My brother and I were tunnel rats. Tunnels were all over the jungle, and our job was to clear them. My brother followed the enemy into a tunnel during a firefight, and before I could follow him, he was gone. I made it into the pit and yelled for him as I crawled deeper into the darkness, and when I finally found him, the enemy had cut his stomach open and left him alive with his guts pulled out. I tried to put it back in and went for help, but when I came back, he was gone. I spent the next six years of my life over there to come back and get spit on by some hippie."

The sheriff paused from his pipe and said, "I lost my nephew and my cousin over there; it was a mess, and I am sorry about your brother, but what does this have to do with Claude Fraley?"

Thomas looked at him and said, "Everything! I have vowed to protect my family, and not all enemies are in foreign lands, and not all people are right. Claude raised his boys to be terrible people; they beat my son—damn near broke his ribs over a football game. I didn't even tell my wife about this!"

The sheriff said, "Yes, I spend my days dealing with wrong people, and the problem here is we have laws which I enforce without malice; you should have contacted this office instead of taking this on yourself. I think you are the right person who just made a dumb choice, and that forces me to do something about it. The way I see it, you have two options. You get up and walk out of here, and by this evening, I will have a warrant out, and you will be thrown away for an extended period, cleaning ditches to cover the expense and effort of bringing you in. The other option is that you stay right here for a few days until the court is held on Thursday. I will keep you until then, and I tell the judge you not only surrendered but cooperated, and we reduce all of this to a misdemeanor with time served—as long as you promise not to use anyone else as a punching bag—and you and your family can continue your life uninterrupted. This means no warrant issued and no official arrest, and it sits as a little more than a parking ticket on your record."

Thomas looked over at the cells and back at the sheriff and said, "What about my job?"

"Hell, I have known Floyd for twenty-five years. I will talk to him personally."

Thomas said, "Will someone contact my wife?"

The sheriff said, "Write your number down, and I will have dispatch contact your home. I am sure your son can comfort your wife and explain what happened. She may be mad at you for not telling her the night this occurred. I bet you thought this would not get to my desk, and it may not have if you had just used your damn sense and called when your boy was beaten up. Now it sounds like you and Claude are even."

Thomas shrugged as he stood up and walked over to the cells. The sheriff unlocked the door, let Thomas in, and closed it behind him. "I will get you a blanket and pillow. You are allowed to use the shower we have in the back, and I don't mind if your wife drops off a change of clothes. We don't have any jumpsuits here; they are over at the jail. You are better off here." Thomas nodded as he sat upon the bed and stared out the window. The sheriff shook his head as he walked over to dispatch and said, "Call his wife and let her know he won't be home for dinner."

FERTILE DIRT STUDIO

The afternoon faded as Jane arrived at the address on the slip from the clerk. As she exited the car and surveyed the old neighborhood, she fixed her eyes on the old porch cracked and worn with vines grown over the surface. A sense of fear and curiosity touched her thoughts. Jane entered the landing at the base of a staircase. To her left was an old door that looked jammed up with wooden slats over the hinges, leaving her only option to walk up. Jane approached the door and ran her fingers over the old brass knob and onto the rough wooden door. As she walked up the stairs, she trembled—not with fear but a curious excitement about what she would find waiting for her at the top of the stairs. When she arrived at the top, she did not hesitate to grab the knob and turn, but the knob did not give. The door was locked.

Jane placed her hands flat against the door, followed by her ear to listen for any activity. Silence then caused her to knock. She turned and began to make her way down the stairs with three brief knocks on the old wooden door. Before she made it three steps, the door opened, and as she turned, she saw the clerk naked with his cock fully erect and the pig mask over his face. Jane smiled as she walked back up the stairs and cupped his balls as she guided his body back through the open doorway into the dimly lit room that was littered with dark sheets over the windows and hanging over adjoining doors. The only light was from candles that flickered about the place, and the shimmer of it peeked over the bed as they met the window's edge.

Jane tugged on the clerk's balls, which brought him to a standstill as she began to shove his enormous cock into her mouth. The man groaned and growled from behind the pig mask as she buried the shaft deep into her throat, squeezing and tugging at his balls as she worked. Now on her knees with her eyes closed, she could feel his cock swelling and throbbing with every glide. Then, finally, Jane opened her eyes as she felt her dress pulled up from the floor behind her. Startled, she stopped sucking and tugging and turned to see another man with his cock right behind her head. He, too, was wearing a pig mask but was much taller and more prominent than the clerk.

Jane stood up and scrambled over to where she found the bed in the dim light and proceeded to remove her clothing. The big pig grabbed her by her slim waist, turning her over as she climbed into bed, shoving his cock in, penetrating her cunt until her ass was against his groin, and forcing her to moan with pleasure as she clawed and grabbed at the mattress. The big pig fucked fast and hard as Jane swallowed cock, sweating as her pussy squeezed tighter and released hot orgasm. Finally, the big pig slid his cock out of Jane, moving off her to allow the clerk to fill her.

The clerk pulled his cock away from Jane's mouth and turned her over on her back, pushing her legs up in the air. He shoved his cock deep into her pink slit and began fucking it rapidly as the big pig stood at the edge of the darkness stroking his monster. The clerk swelled and throbbed as he plunged in her, gasping and grunting as his nuts tingled. The big pig came from the edge of the room; stepping behind the clerk, he placed his hand on the back of the clerk and motioned him to bend over.

The clerk leaned forward as he continued to fuck, and the big pig proceeded to slide his cock into the clerk's asshole. So, the clerk was almost on top of Jane, working her, as the big pig was hip to hip in the same motion as the clerk, buried deep inside him. This went on for several minutes before the clerk stopped fucking and turned his head to nod at the big pig. The big pig pulled out of the clerk's ass and backed up. The clerk then pulled out of Jane as she sat up. The clerk stuck his cock in her face, rubbing his head against her lips. She began to suck as the clerk tensed up. Jane grabbed the clerk's balls and squeezed as the clerk moaned and released his load into her mouth. She sucked it all down, not missing a single drop. Finally, the clerk stepped back, removing his cock from her mouth, and stepping into the darkness.

Jane turned her attention to the big pig as he approached her. The big pig motioned with his hand for Jane to turn over. She complied and got on her knees as the big pig removed his mask and revealed the face of a man younger than her. The man spat on his hand, rubbed it on his cock, and then penetrated her asshole. Not just with the tip but all the way down until their hips were connected. Jane was overcome with pain and pleasure while she orgasmed and shook as he worked in and out the several inches of cock into her. Jane bit into a pillow as the man fucked more laboriously and more profoundly. She moaned and shrieked as it felt like he was splitting her. The man pulled out of her as Jane turned; he grabbed her, leaning her head to his cock as he exploded hot cum all over her. As she fell back on the bed covered in his load, the clerk appeared with a pig mask, and before she realized what was happening, Jane had a needle in her shoulder and felt dizzy before blacking out. The clerk placed the pig mask over Jane's cum-covered face, and both men left the room.

Tim made it home and walked into the house to find it entirely empty as if the world stopped. No Mom, no dad, no sister. Tim walked up the stairs to his room and closed the door. Closing his eyes for a moment at rest, he leaned the back of his head on the wall. He remembered the cigarettes as he looked down at the floor and cracked a smile. He carefully removed the loose board from the floor and opened the flap in the carton to reveal the cigarettes. He grabbed a box and removed one cigarette, then paused with a smile before removing another to place it in his ear. He returned the pack to the floor, put the board back, grabbed his matches from his dresser, left his room, walked down the hall, and looked out at the roof over the back porch.

Opening the window, he slid out onto the roof and sat with his back against the corner. He lit up and inhaled, watching the smoke drift away in the air. Looking around with each puff, he made sure he was not seen. He finished his last drag and leaned forward to drop the butt into the gutter. Tim turned and climbed back in the window. The phone rang in the kitchen as Tim made his way downstairs and answered. On the other end, the dispatch asked for Jane. Tim replied, "She is not home yet."

The dispatch informed Tim that his mom needed to call the sheriff's office, and when Tim asked if everything was OK, the dispatch replied, "Please have your mom call as soon as she can."

Tim sat at the table in the quiet house alone with his thoughts, thinking this must be because of what Dad did to Fraley. I hope Dad is all right. Is this my fault? I should have been tougher. All of this is because of Susie. I know this is on the Fraley brothers. They are older; they should have known better than to hurt me over a football game. They see me as a queer. Is that how others see me? Do Ricky and I seem gay to other kids? Maybe I need to get a girlfriend. I am just too shy to ask. Perhaps I need to stop covering for my sister, give up the cigarettes, and spend more time with Susie. Tim laid his head on his arms and rested at the table, hoping to calm his mind.

Molly arrived home to find a quiet house and began the family search. Molly entered the kitchen to find Tim sleeping at the table; she walked over and shook his shoulder as she said, "Hey, Tim, get up."

Tim raised his head and said, "What time is it?"

Molly replied, "It's a little after five o'clock. Where is Mom or Dad?"

Tim replied, "Where have you been, more prom planning with Johnny?" as he smiled. Molly rolled her eyes as she looked at Tim, and he remembered the phone call. "Shit!" Tim said, "I think Dad is at the sheriff station!" Molly sat beside Tim to hear the rest.

Molly said, "Do you think Dad found out about Johnny?"

"No, dummy!" Tim said. "Not everything is about you and Johnny!"

Molly frowned as she looked at Tim and said, "Well, what then?"

Tim proceeded to tell Molly what happened after he got beat up when he left with Dad before the trip to the emergency room. "I think it has something to do with what Dad did to Claude Fraley. He was rude to Dad, and the boys called me gay, and Dad beat Mr. Fraley bad. I don't know what else it could be."

Molly paused and sighed in relief, "At least it wasn't about Johnny."

Tim replied, "That's right because it's always about you, and that is all that matters." Tim got up and continued, "You are such a stupid sister, and I am not covering for you anymore!"

Molly responded, "Well, maybe I just go live with Johnny now, or we leave this shitty little town!" Molly got up, slammed the chair, and walked out of the kitchen and out the front door to sit on the porch swing. Tim got up and went up to his room to lay on his bed.

Jane regained consciousness and opened her eyes as she pulled the mask off her face. Startled by events, she got up, still dizzy from the shot, and found her clothes. Before the men returned, she got dressed quickly and made her way down the dark stairs and onto the street. She looked back at the old house as she got into her car and drove off toward home. Looking at the watch on her wrist, Jane realized it was two-thirty in the morning. She never made it home and never made it to work. She turned on her street and pulled into the house slowly relieved but curious when she noticed the truck was gone. Was Thomas looking for her or was he at the bar?

She hoped the latter as she quietly walked into the house with her clothing bags. Looking around the still empty house, she made her way down the hall and placed her bags in the bedroom before heading off to the shower. Taking off her clothes and throwing them in the trash can, Jane stepped in under the water and rubbed her ravaged body as thoughts of her adventure filled her mind. Owning her foolishness and without self-pity, Jane soaped herself free of the filth and rinsed herself clean. Sore from being worked hard, she felt her arm where the needle went and wondered why they drugged her.

Then she decided to hurry as to not be caught by Thomas and forced into answering questions. She turned off the water and grabbed her towel, dried off, then slipped into the pajamas from the closet. After looking at her arm in the mirror, she walked down the hall, pulled back the blankets, and crawled into bed. Adjusting her pillows and clicking the night light off, she lay in the darkness, overcome with joy that she just got fucked beyond her wildest fantasy and got away with it. This thought was her last as she drifted away into sleep.

Sleep was the last thing Thomas was getting as he lay on the bed in the cell, and the light coming from the streetlamp outside illuminated a spot on the floor that extended its way onto the green linen that covered him. The dispatch sat quietly at her desk, the only sound the hum of the radio and her picking through the local paper. Just as Thomas was ready to turn away from the dispatch and the light and face toward the bars of the other cell, dark and still, feeling the drift of sleep reach his brain, he was startled and wrestled back to consciousness by a slam of the office's front door.

Thomas sat up and looked in the direction of the noise to see two deputies sitting next to the dispatcher at the desk. The dispatch stated, "Walton and Mills, it seems I have a message from the sheriff for you two. It reads that you are both supposed to be on patrol over by the Walton Farm."

Mills and Walton shrugged and looked at the dispatcher, and Walton remarked, "What's the hurry? Besides, we think we got one of the offenders in there when we picked him up for trespassing. The other one maybe has something to do with this?"

Thomas's jaw tightened as he turned and stared directly at Walton, wanting to reply. Walton noticed his stare and said, "What's a matter, boy? You don't want to talk?" Mills leaned back, placing his hands behind his head, and smiling as he got ready to watch the show. Walton stood up, walked over to the cell, and said to Thomas, "Wait a minute. I know you; your son is that queer that could not fight his own fights, so you had to fight for him." The dispatcher turned and stared directly at the radio to avoid being bullied by Walton.

The deputy smiled at Thomas. "I know Claude Fraley. Heck, I was the one he contacted after you beat him up. I was the one that helped him, and his boys get to the hospital. I told him to contact the sheriff, and then I told the sheriff to bring you here and to go easy on you just so I could make your stay miserable. I know your son is queer. Are you queer too?" Mills smiled and laughed as Walton continued to ramble, and Thomas remained silent. Walton looked at Thomas and said, "How about I stick my dick through the bars and let you have a suck? Hell, you could take care of both of us!" Mills continued to laugh.

Walton walked to the bars, unzipped his pants, and pulled out his cock. "Come on, queer, now is your chance." Thomas slid on the bed away from Walton and turned his head away. Walton began to piss on the cell floor as he smiled at Thomas.

The dispatcher finally turned her head toward the two deputies and said, "It is three in the damn morning, and I am calling Sheriff Davis!" She began to dial the phone as Walton put his cock away and walked over to her desk and grabbed the receiver from her hand, followed by Mills getting up from the chair to follow behind Walton.

The dispatcher said, "Let go of this receiver, or I will tell the sheriff everything in the morning, and you two will be fired by tomorrow and may end up in that cell too!"

Walton let go of the receiver and said, "Come on, Mills. Let's go patrol." Walton turned and looked at Thomas, who watched the events unfold and said, "Don't you have some piss to clean up?" The two deputies left the same way they came in, leaving only Thomas, the dispatcher, and the man in the bed across from him.

The dispatcher frowned at Thomas and said, "I am sorry." Thomas shrugged as he rubbed his forehead and looked down at the piss-covered tile. "I have heard about you," the dispatcher said. "I don't believe you are a terrible person, and if it were my son, I would have done the same thing."

Thomas looked up as he replied, "Thank you."

The dispatch said, "Don't worry about those two idiots; maybe they will shoot each other."

Thomas smiled and mumbled, "Only a few nights."

The dispatch said, "My name is Wanda, by the way, Wanda Trickle, but everyone calls me Trixie." Trixie looked at Thomas and indicated, "If you promise not to escape, I have the keys to the cell and a mop bucket. We can clean up the mess. I will get you some fresh clothes and let you change in the restroom." Trixie walked down the hall into the dark and returned with a mop and bucket, dangling some keys.

Thomas agreed. "What about him?" Thomas gestured as he looked over at the man sleeping on the other bed.

"He hasn't moved since they brought him last night. I think he has a nasty hangover." Trixie unlocked the door and pushed the mop and bucket into the cell. Thomas took the mop and began to clean up the mess. Trixie stood with the cell door unlocked but closed until Thomas finished off the floor. Trixie opened the door, letting Thomas out, and locked it behind him. Thomas pushed the bucket down the hall as he followed Trixie to the restroom. Trixie opened a locker, pulled out a towel, some soap, a washcloth, and a blue jumpsuit. She smiled and said, "The sheriff isn't in charge of inventory; I am, and I have these just in case." Trixie handed the items to Thomas and proceeded to sit in a chair outside the restroom door. Thomas went into the restroom to get cleaned up.

RUNAWAY

The deputies parked the cruiser at the back of Billy Walton's farm at the base of the hill with the orchard beyond. Mills rolled down the window as the night air rushed in.

"I sure showed that dumb ass Stover, didn't I?" Walton said as Mills nodded his head.

Then Mills said, "What about Trixie?"

Walton replied," If she talks, we know where she lives. We will round her up and take turns on her." Walton grabbed his cock and looked at Mills and said, "But I go first!"

Mills looked out the window at the moon as it floated in and out of the clouds. "What are we really doing out here?" Mills said as he turned and looked at Walton. "I mean, do you think it's really some kind of cult?" Mills looked back out the window at the moon and said, "I just think it's some hillbilly hippies with some animals having an orgy."

Walton said, "I think it's just a bunch of stupid fucks wasting our time! I could be out pulling young girls over just to scare them into taking off their panties!"

Mills said, "Does that work?"

Walton said, "Get out of the car. I want to show you something."

Walton and Mills got out of the vehicle, and Walton walked around to the trunk. "I found this stepping out of town before I picked you up tonight." Walton opened the trunk and revealed a teenage girl gagged and tied up. "She told me she was running away, and I threatened to take her to jail. I told her to get in the trunk and tied her up." Walton looked at Mills and said, "Now we are going to fuck her!"

Mills hesitated and looked at Walton and said, "What?"

Walton said, "Don't worry. She's eighteen and has identification, which means she is old enough, and when we are done, we will let her go, and if she talks, she disappears."

Walton said, "Now help me get her out and get hard because we are about to fuck!"

Mills complied and helped Walton pull the girl out of the trunk and bend her over, still gagged and tied. The girl struggled to get free and began to cry. Walton pushed her head into the open trunk, bending her over the car's back, and Mills helped and held her steady. Walton undid her pants and panties as he pulled them down to her feet. Walton removed his gun belt, throwing it down on the ground. Walton told Mills to hold the girl steady as he unzipped his pants, pulling out his erection and slipping it in the girl. Walton began to push and pump as the girl squirmed, and Mills held on. Walton spoke between grunting and pumping, "This isn't so bad, is it, baby?" as the girl continued to cry. "Do not worry, Mills. I won't smash this up too bad," Walton began to say and then stopped suddenly, pulling out his cock and stroking it as he stiffened his body to release his nut on the ground.

"Goddamn, that is some tight shit, girl. You could make some money off a snatch like that." Walton put his dirty cock back in his pants and zipped them shut, grabbing his belt from the ground as Mills continued to hold the girl, who had stopped crying and squirming, a sense of defeat entering her mind. "Well, shit, my pants," Walton said as he touched his own cum that landed on his belt. "Not only did I fuck her into submission, but I shot my belt." Walton laughed as he wiped the sticky cum on the girl's back and proceeded to hold her down.

The girl tried to speak through the gag before Mills got ready for his shot. Mills said to Walton, "Is she trying to say something?"

"Of course, she is," said Walton. "We have her in our control, and she knows it. Well, let us just see what she has to say." Walton stood the girl up as Mills removed the gag.

The girl said, "You two aren't the first to use me," as she looked at the men. "Why do you think I was running away?" The girl looked at Mills and said, "You do not want my pussy after he has been in me, but I can suck your cock good. I will even swallow, so you don't get it on you. But, if I do this, please let me go, and I will not tell anyone. I just want to leave this shitty town!"

Walton looked at the girl and said, "No funny stuff here; you take care of my partner, and I will let you go. If you even think of trying anything or telling anyone about this, I am related to everyone in this county. I will find you, and I will kill you!" The girl's eyes widened in fear as she nodded in agreement.

"Could you please untie my hands so I can use them?" she asked. Walton took a knife out of his belt and carefully cut the rope from the girl's wrists and then placed the knife back in his belt and placed his hand on his gun handle.

"Now, go ahead, suck!" Walton said as he looked back at the girl. The girl sat on the bumper of the squad car and looked up at Mills, and replied, "Are you ready for me?" The girl unbuttoned Mills's pants and unzipped them, revealing his boxers.

She then took her hands and pulled his pants and boxers to his knees, exposing his cock. "My God!" she said with surprise, "That is a huge dick! I should have kept quiet and let you fuck me with that thing!" Mills smiled as the girl looked up at him, placed her mouth on to his head, and worked down the shaft. He gasped as she gagged a bit before running her mouth all the way down to his balls, pushing the cock into her throat. She worked her head up and down as the deputy closed his eyes and leaned his head back.

Walton watched, still resting on the gun as he smiled in approval at her effort. Mills got harder and grabbed her head and began to direct her motion as she slobbered and gagged on his penis. Mills pulled her hair back and said, "Hold on a minute." The girl stopped and looked up at Mills, and he said as he looked down at her, "I want you to put your feet on the bumper!" He guided her legs to where he wanted them. Mills leaned forward with her legs now wide open and penetrated her with his long cock. He began to drive deep and hard as he placed her hands on his shoulders and rocked the squad car with his thrust. The girl started to moan as Mills worked harder to fuck her.

Walton began to get aroused and felt his erection hardening for another round. Walton took his hand off his gun and removed his cock again with excitement. He looked at Mills as he fucked and pushed him aside, taking his place. Mills fell from the push, landing on the ground, startled with his erection sticking straight up and his pants tangled between his shoes and belt. Walton grabbed the girl by the throat as he fucked as hard and as fast as he could. She opened her eyes and watched his face as he fucked and choked her.

Walton could feel his nuts begin to tighten as he was ready to cum again. The girl felt the deputy getting close and reached for the gun on his belt. Walton sensed her hand tugging at the holster, backed out of her, drew his weapon, and shot the girl in the forehead, spraying the trunk of the car with blood, bone, and brains. Walton placed the gun back in the holster and said to Mills, "Get up, you dumb shit. I was going to kill this bitch anyway!" Walton proceeded to grab his still erect cock and jerk off until he nut again before wiping his hand on the grass and putting his cock away. Mills scrambled to get untangled and to his feet, finally getting his pants and belt back where they belong, the whole time in shock from what he just witnessed. "You just killed that girl! What the hell are we going to do now?"

Walton looked at Mills and said, "She went for my gun, so shut up and help me put her back in the trunk!" The two deputies placed the bloody body in the trunk, shutting the lid and getting in the cruiser.

"Now what?" Mills said as the shock turned to panic.

Walton said, "No worries. I know just the place to dump her, and it's only on the other side of this hill."

Walton started the car and drove down a dirt path past the rows of corn to a place where the field ended. The two deputies got out and removed the body from the trunk, carrying it up a slight rise to a hole in the ground. Walton said, "We call this 'Martha'—this old sinkhole where my cousin dumps all of the guts from the hogs he butchers." Mills and Walton laid the corpse on the ground and slid it down into the hole until it disappeared into the darkness; several seconds passed, and the echo of the body hitting the bottom reached the two deputies.

Walton said, "This is a deep hole. Tell anyone about this, and you will end up right here!"

Mills said, "What about all the blood and brains in the trunk?"

Walton reasoned, "We can take it out to my barn and clean it up. I have a power washer. That way we can keep it out of town. We can burn our uniforms. I have some extras at my place just for occasions like this."

Mills looked at Walton and said, "Have you done this before?"

Walton smiled and implied, "I stuff Martha's stinky hole well, and what do you think happened to my last partner?" Mills looked at the hole and back at Walton and nodded out of fear and discomfort.

Mills asked, "What about the sheriff?"

Walton smiled and said, "That old fuck doesn't know a thing! I have been doing this for years. All this devil worship nonsense just helps me out. Besides, Davis will not be sheriff forever, and soon I will be in charge, and if you want along for the ride, just follow along."

Mills looked at Walton and said, "What about the special investigator from the city?"

Walton smiled and said, "All we need to do is apply some misdirection to help him catch someone to make a few arrests and go away. People go missing all the time, and if someone really cared, they wouldn't go missing in the first place." Mills smiled and nodded his head as Walton got up and led him down the hill. The deputies got into the cruiser and drove out of the path from the Martha and onto the road.

Tim and Molly made their way down the stairs to leave for school. Molly walked through the kitchen and out the back door without so much as a goodbye to Tim as he watched her go, closing the door behind her. He walked to the front door of the house to gather his jean jacket and stuff the inner pocket with cigarettes before noticing Jane's wagon sitting in the driveway.

Tim realized that his mom may not know about Dad and was not sure what she was doing at home. Tim walked down the hallway to his parents' room and gently opened the door just enough to whisper into the room. "Mom, are you awake? I need to talk to you," Tim whispered as he faced the door frame with his hand resting on the knob. Tim whispered again, this time just a little bit louder. "Mom, I need to talk to you!"

Finally, a voice came from the other side of the door. "I am awake now, Tim; come on in." Tim entered the room and looked at Jane and then looked at the empty side of the bed where Dad typically slept.

Jane said, "Come sit," as she moved her legs over and looked at Tim's eyes as he looked at the other side of the bed.

Tim sat and said," Mom, that night Dad took me to the hospital, we stopped at Claude Fraley's house. His boys were the ones that beat me up."

Mom paused and said, "OK, maybe your dad forgot to tell me. It was a busy night."

"No, Mom. Dad told me not to say anything to you because he beat Claude really bad, and yesterday when you weren't home, the sheriff's office called, and I think Dad is in jail for it. This is all my fault for not coming straight home and not being able to fight back."

Jane sat up and said, "You did nothing wrong. I will handle this with your father; now go on to school, and I will be home when you return, and we can talk about all of this then." Tim stood up and looked at Mom and said, "Where were you yesterday?" Jane saw an image of the two men from yesterday briefly flash through her mind before responding.

"I went shopping for new uniforms for work then drove by here, didn't see the truck, and was worried about your father. I drove around looking for him, which didn't provide me any time to rest, so I stopped by the hospital again and talked to Dr. Brady and took the night off."

Tim smiled and said, "Dr. Brady was the one that took care of me the other night. He seems like a smart doctor."

Jane smiled and said, "Yes, and I will visit your father and won't tell him we talked." Tim gave his mom a hug, got up, and walked out of the bedroom, waving to his mother. Jane stretched as she thought to herself, processing all the lies she had been telling her family to organize them in her mind to keep them straight. Jane got up out of bed and made her way down the hall to start her day.

Tim strolled to school, weary of the recent events hanging over him. The fear of another run-in with the Fraley brothers caused his hands to tremble. The feelings turned to anxiety as he stopped at the crosswalk and looked at the school building and all the students and traffic and noise surrounding him. Tim wished his sister would have walked with him and that she was not mad at him. He sighed as he walked across the street, passing other children, cutting through the noise, and going numb to block out his surroundings. Tim took one last look over his shoulder before opening the wooden double doors and venturing into the school, cutting his way through the busy hallway.

Sheriff Davis arrived at the office, slowly getting out of his cruiser, adjusting his belt, and burping up bacon from the morning meal at home. Trixie sat at the dispatch desk handing information over to her daytime relief. The two men in the cells down the hall laid sleeping on their beds as the sheriff walked in. The sheriff greeted Trixie, and she said good morning before walking out the door to end her shift. The sheriff walked over to the cells and noticed the blue jumpsuit on Thomas's leg and both men's stillness. The sheriff asked the dispatcher, "Did Trixie say anything about his change of clothes?" The dispatcher said that she was told he missed the toilet and pissed on the floor and himself last night.

The sheriff sighed as he noticed Thomas's clothes folded up under the bed. The sheriff went to his desk and said, "Any check-in from my two deputies?"

The dispatch said, "Nothing yet, sir." The sheriff shook his head and reached for his pipe. He then propped his feet up and relaxed for a smoke. The door to the sheriff station opened and in walked a man to the dispatch desk. The man looked around the small office and noticed the old, occupied cells down the hall before addressing the dispatcher.

"Good morning. My name is Martin Donnell. I am the state special investigator from the Toledo office. I am here to see Sheriff Davis." The sheriff, taking notice from his office, put his pipe down and took his feet off the desk.

"You can send him in to see me," the sheriff said.

The dispatcher smiled at Martin and said, "The sheriff will see you now." The sheriff stood up to greet Martin as he entered the office, and the two men shook hands. Martin sat opposite the sheriff in the tiny office and began his introduction.

"My name is Martin Donnell. I am a special investigator from Toledo, as requested. How can I help your county, Sheriff?"

Davis pushed a stack of files over to Martin and said, "We are a small department, and I save this county money by keeping it that way, but that means we don't have the resources to investigate missing persons or strange activity like some of the more populated counties. I currently have four active deputies and three dispatchers. My two daytime deputies are presently working overnight to cover a new scene of cult activity, and my afternoon deputies are taking care of everything else. I had a fifth deputy that disappeared over the summer without notice, but he had a gambling problem, and we worry he got in with the wrong kind of debt. Currently, this year alone, we have had an additional twelve missing persons, women ranging in age from sixteen all the way to thirty and a few teenage boys." Sheriff Davis paused and said, "At first, I thought it was nothing because people go missing all the time for one reason or another. It doesn't mean homicide, but the cases slowly increased, and then we have all of this local cult activity on these rural farms as recently as the other night, so my fear is we have something genuinely evil taking place here."

Martin looked at the sheriff and said, "Well, we have no time to waste. I will call in additional support, and I say we get started right now. I need you to take me to where this last round of reported cult activity took place." The sheriff agreed, and the two men left the office and got into the sheriff's cruiser, leaving the sheriff department.

Jane stepped into the shower, and she began to wash her body. Her hand glided the washcloth to her ass as she paused in soreness. She rubbed the spot on her ass as she tried to see the source of the pain. Jane finished up quickly and exited the steamy shower. She grabbed the hand mirror from her vanity and placed it at an angle below her left ass cheek off to the side and looked down to see a series of deep scratches. The scratches appeared straight-lined, almost in a pattern, but Jane could only see parts of it from the small mirror. Jane sighed as it seemed this must have occurred when she was knocked out. "How will I lie out of this one?" Jane said to herself as she began to get dressed.

Thomas awakened at the sound of a sliding noise across the floor. He sat up and looked for the source of the sound. Thomas noticed two plates of food on the floor by the dispatcher, who stood up and walked down the hall to her desk. Unfortunately, this was not the dispatcher that helped him out last night. She seemed evasive, avoiding eye contact, as she sat back at her office, keeping her head on the radio as she began to eat an apple. Thomas looked over at the other man, still sleeping on his bed, and since he would get no help from the dispatcher, he decided to wake him up. Thomas looked at the man and stood up to tap him on the shoulder. Thomas stepped slowly with his hand outstretched to place it on the man's shoulder, but with his third step, the man sat up, brushed his black hair from his eyes, looked at Thomas, and turned toward the plates of food on the floor. He picked up both and handed one to Thomas without so much as a word as he scooped the food with his large hand, mashing it all together into his mouth.

Thomas paused to watch before starting his own plate. The man looked up from his plate, and his dark eyes looked like two pieces of coal shining on his tan face. As he ate, the man said to Thomas, "Are you going to eat or not?"

Thomas looked at his plate before handing it to the man. "My name is Thomas."

The man smiled as he put his empty plate beside him and grabbed it from Thomas. "My name is Ayaz."

Thomas said, "How did you end up here?"

"I was hunting after dark."

"Poaching?" Thomas said as he raised an eyebrow.

"No, I was hunting," Ayaz said. "I crossed over a farm and ran into some deputies who said I did not belong there. They took my rifle and locked me up." Ayaz looked at Thomas and said, "Now what about you?"

Thomas said, "I beat a man whose boys beat my son."

Ayaz nodded his head and said "Zorba." Thomas looked puzzled as Ayaz said, "I am Turkish, and *Zorba* is what you call a bully."

Thomas said, "Well, you're a long, long way from Turkey just to hunt."

Ayaz nodded and said, "A lot to kill." Thomas sat with his back against the bars and placed his hand on his brow to think. Ayaz began to eat the food that Thomas gave to him, finishing in a few scoops out of his hand. Ayaz placed both plates on the floor, slid them out of the cell with his leg turned, looked over his shoulder, and said, "I have to shit." The dispatch looked up from her desk and snickered as she smiled and took a bite out of her apple.

The sheriff and Donnell walked up the hill to the tree where the cult had been. Donnell examined the tree and looked at the fire pit and surrounding area. The sheriff said, "Now you see what we are up against."

Donnell kneeled down to examine the ground and said, "I have been through this before. I am from a rural area, just like this one. I formerly come from Schuylkill County, Pennsylvania, or 'Kill County' as I call it. My father was a bank manager there. The town prospered because of the local mine that had been there since the end of the Civil War."

Donnell paused as he surveyed the hilltop perimeter. Donnell continued to talk as the sheriff stood by, listening. "I was a young detective in Eerie County when my father was gunned down in a robbery. I went back home to help the local sheriff, who I had known since I was a kid, solve my father's murder. The mine folded, the bank closed, and the town died as well. I finally caught up with those responsible in a cabin up in the hills, but when I found them, they were already dead, and the money was never recovered. The locals would say it was a curse from some freed slave descendants that cursed the robbers with dark magic. I just think that the town was cursed. Last year, another small town in

Ohio had problems with cult activity, and it made it all the way to the president, and we evacuated. My point is, Sheriff, evil is accurate, and once again, I will do all I can to help this county and its people." Donnell stood back up and pointed to a path on the other side of the field.

The sheriff looked on and said, "That leads to an old sinkhole. Locals use it to dump butchered leftovers from livestock."

Donnell looked at the sheriff and said, "I want to see that; let's check it out."

Jane pulled up to the sheriff's department, took a deep breath, and looked in her rearview mirror to practice a smile before getting out of the wagon. Jane walked into the sheriff's station, stopped at the dispatch, and asked to see Thomas Stover. Thomas opened his eyes as Jane approached the cell. The dispatcher said, "Don't cross the line!" as Jane looked down at the yellow stripe painted around the cell's perimeter. Jane frowned as she stepped to the edge and looked at Thomas. Thomas stood up as he looked over at Ayaz and said, "Hey, Turk, my wife, Jane. Jane, meet Turk." Ayaz smiled as the nickname took his mind off his stomach pain from all that breakfast.

Jane, pretending she needed an update, asked Thomas what happened. Thomas said, "My temper got the best of me, and they wanted to make sure that it does not occur again. How are the kids?"

Jane smiled and said, "They miss their dad."

Thomas said, "Just a few more days, and the sheriff said as long as I behave, I will be out of here. My truck is still at work; that is where Davis met me."

Jane looked at Thomas and said, "I need to cancel my convention trip this weekend."

Thomas said, "No worries. I will be useful, and I promise I will be home by the time the kids get off school on Thursday."

The dispatcher looked at Jane and said, "OK, your time is up; you can come back tomorrow." Jane turned and looked at the dispatch and looked back at Thomas as she told him she loved him. Thomas nodded and smiled as he watched Jane turn and walk out the door. Jane got in her car, and as she sat the pain from the cuts on her cheek caused her some discomfort. Jane decided to take her frustration out on the clerk who fucked her and cut her. Jane, now on a mission, headed in the direction of the shop.

Sheriff Davis and Donnell stood at the opening to the sinkhole. Donnell said, "Damn, this is a big hole," as he tried to size up the opening, walking around the sinkhole. Donnell stopped and said to Davis, "We need a team to search this hole. I have blood here, and I would like it tested." Donnell looked at Davis and said, "This is now a crime scene. We need to leave until my team can come and examine this whole area and all the surrounding farms; this is now a state investigation. Please have all your deputies cease all investigations unless I give the direction. I will expect full cooperation."

Sheriff Davis looked back at Donnell and said, "I have been sheriff here for twenty-seven years, and I have to admit this is the first time I have seen this type of activity. Something has changed, and I agree with what you said on the hill about evil, and I am worried about the county and the darkness." The two men headed down to the cruiser.

MARTHA

Martha Perkins sat at her desk as she focused on the number of corrections, she made on each student assignment. Her red hair rested just slightly beyond her shoulders, matched by her bright lipstick. The maroon blouse rose just above her shoulders, exposing the tops of her breasts. Her well-kept, thirty-something body made her the focus of many young seniors. The class was quietly working along with the occasional murmur from one student to the next. Martha occasionally looked up at the students to make sure they were staying on task.

It was during those inspections that she caught the attention of Billy Walton. Billy smiled from the front row of the class as she looked on. Martha looked back down at her work as she wondered if he knew about her. She began to daydream about all the young men she had sucked on. This made Martha wet as she shifted in her chair, closing her legs tighter. The reasoning of her actions made sense to her. It satisfied her want to have power over young men as she made them cum—the return for each passing grade. Would Billy Walton be her next? she thought as she looked back at him. She turned her attention to his pants and noticed the bulge between his open legs.

Looking back at the papers to find his assignment, she shuffled quickly through the documents. The inspection revealed that his schoolwork contained no labor, just his name at the top. She looked up at Billy and cleared her throat too, and the decision was made to call him from the class. Billy stood up and smiled as he strutted to her desk and leaned forward to engage.

"Billy," Martha whispered, "why is this assignment incomplete?"

Billy whispered back as he stood straight up and said, "You know why."

Martha said, "Then see me after class." Billy nodded as she looked back at the classroom to make certain no one was paying attention. Then he returned to his seat and continued his assignment. Martha continued to grade papers as a sense of excitement filled her mind. The clock seemed to move even slower, almost standing still before the final bell for the day landed. The classroom emptied as Martha smiled and said goodbye to all the students for the weekend. Finally, the moment had arrived; it was just Martha and Billy. Martha sat back and uncrossed her legs as Billy stood to face her with his back to the hallway door.

Martha smiled and announced, "If you want to pass my class, you know what I expect." Billy looked down at Martha and raised his eyebrows as he unzipped his pants just enough to expose the head of his cock. Martha became hot as she looked around at the empty room before turning her attention back to the throbbing purple head.

Billy tucked it back in his pants and said, "Meet me tonight behind my parents' farm, and you can have all you want." Martha nodded in quick response to his gesture as Billy turned to walk out of the room.

Martha got up to follow Billy and shut the door to the classroom, leaving her time alone with her thoughts. She sat back at her desk as she slid her chair forward and slid her hand under her skirt, placing her fingers in her wet pussy. She worked back and forth with them as she thought about young Billy penetrating her. This made her cum rapidly as she grabbed the desk with her other hand before letting out a moan. Martha then removed her fingers, and her ecstasy turned to sadness as she noticed the smell.

Martha was reminded why she only sucked cock and fingered herself for pleasure. The odor of her pussy was strong and most foul—the kind of smell that would keep anyone from wanting in. Martha began to recount her days during the war when she was a USO party girl who was fucked by soldiers before going to the jungle to die. The many cocks ruined her, she affirmed in her mind. She was young and used that Saigon money to pay for her education. Martha sat at her desk, wiping her cum on to tissue before placing it in the trash. She smiled again as she relaxed back, happy because of all the of cocks her lips had stroked, the young men whose loads she gulped for the satisfaction of having control over them, and all the fantasies secured firmly in her mind. Martha closed her folder of grading papers, grabbed her purse, and walked out of the classroom, leaving an open door for the janitor to clean.

The janitor from around the corner watched Martha as she left. He entered her classroom. Placing his cleaning cart against the wall underneath the blackboard, he proceeded to pick up the trash can to empty into his cart. The smell took of rot like a dead fish in the sun and filled up his nostrils. He quickly dumped the trash into his carriage before returning it to the floor. He then grabbed for his broom, shaking his head while he began to hum and sweep.

Martha arrived at her flat, entering only to head straight for the shower. She stripped to nothing, showing off her fit, young body. The warm water flowed over her as she gently cleaned her vagina, sliding the soap and cloth over her smooth lips. The shower was followed by a tight red dress with no panties or bra. Martha grabbed the perfume from the counter as she finished her hair and lipstick, spraying her inner thighs and vagina to help disguise the inevitable return of her odor. Her mind, for a moment, floated the idea of maybe going to the doctor.

The thought immediately caused her to shake her head as she looked in the mirror. The logic of being embarrassed, being labeled a whore, and becoming gossip in this small town was enough to settle her thoughts. Martha turned and walked out of the bathroom to retrieve her keys and purse before walking out the door.

The sunset brought Billy Walton down the path to the old hog barn just over the hill from home. He made his way past the rows of hog pens before entering the old office. The anticipation of Martha's arrival had him both nervous and excited. Billy sat on a wooden chair that creaked as he seated himself. Billy rubbed his pants over his cock and felt his erection building. The tight jeans did not have enough room for his growing cock. Billy unzipped his pants and exposed his stiff meat as he began to stroke it with anticipation. He jumped off the seat, startled as he caught Martha watching from the corner of his eye. "How long have you been there?" he asked as Martha smiled.

"I watched as I walked in the barn from the woods where I parked my car, so it looks like I arrived just in time." Martha turned the chair toward Billy and sat. "Here," she said, "let me help you with that." She grabbed his cock and slowly placed her lips over the head.

Billy trembled with excitement of her head bobbing up and down, running her mouth the length of his shaft. Martha stopped and looked up at Billy and said, "You have a nice cock. I think we could have some real fun this year," before placing her tongue on the tip and licking around the head.

Billy looked down as he gasped at the pleasure. "Mrs. Perkins, let me fuck you," he said in a low voice. Martha ignored the request as she continued to suck. Billy placed his hands on Martha's shoulders as he pushed her away from him.

Martha stood up and said, "This is over!" as she turned and walked away, leaving Billy hard and frustrated. Martha made it past the rows of hogs before Billy grabbed her from behind, guiding her over to some railing that was waist high from the floor. Martha grabbed the railing in excitement as Billy pushed up her dress, revealing her soft white skin and skinny ass. Billy found her pussy with his cock and pushed. Martha shrieked in pleasure as Billy fucked quickly. He shook the rail with a powerful thrust. Billy thrusted harder as he could feel his load building. Martha began to quiver as her cum ran down her leg. Billy gave one last hard thrust as he filled Martha with his orgasm. Martha turned around, pulling down her dress, as Billy put his softening erection back into his pants.

Martha looked in disbelief; walked out of the barn into the darkness toward the woods and her car. Billy walked back the way he had come as a feeling of power and satisfaction consumed his thoughts. The house was dark as Billy made his way up the stairs to the bathroom. He turned the water on to let it heat up as he readied himself for a shower. Stripping off his clothes, he stopped as he slid his underwear to his knees. He examined the dampness of his penis and caught the smell. Puzzled and disturbed, he finished removing his drawers and stepped into the shower. Billy washed and scrubbed, eliminating all traces of his activity. He dried off and examined himself before climbing into bed and turning off the lamp.

Martha sat on her closed porch in her robe, covering her freshly showered body, and she looked out into the night while she sipped her tea with lemon. The feeling of being fucked was still with her, but the concern overshadowed the ecstasy. *He for sure had to have smelled it*, she thought to herself. *My dirty slit is very noticeable; it always smells*, she thought as she opened her robe. She slid one finger past her clit and into her hole. Removing it, she placed it to her nose to get a scent. The smell was sufficient to make her cry as she stuck the finger in the last of her tea to rinse the foul odor. *The doctor*, she thought, *Monday I will go to the doctor.* Martha wiped her tears as she got up and made her way to bed. She was thinking only of Billy and his cock as she held hope that maybe he did not notice.

—

The morning always started early on the farm. Billy rose from his bed before the rise of the early morning sun. He was cloaked in the dim morning light as he made his way down the hallway into the bathroom. Billy let the cold-water flow from the faucet as he splashed his face. The flow stopped as Billy turned the water off and lifted the toilet seat to piss. The morning piss felt good after the fuck he had last night. Billy smiled as he thought of himself as a teacher-fucker. Placing his penis back into his drawers and reaching to turn the water on to wash his hands, his nose caught something peculiar. That smell from last night's encounter was still present. He could smell it on his hands as he works to scrub it off. Billy dried his hands and got dressed, avoiding any breakfast as he went out the back door on his way to feed the hogs.

Martha woke up with concern on her mind. The nervousness caused her to get dressed, and before she knew it, she found herself sitting in her car, contemplating her next move. The decision was final. She would check on Billy and make it a homework follow-up to avoid any parental suspicion of her activity. The car ride was brief as Martha parked in the woods and waited to hopefully see Billy before going to the house and inquiring. The slow sunrise assisted as Martha noticed a tractor slowly creeping up the hill that separates the farm from the woods. Martha got out of her car and walked in the tractor's direction. Losing sight of it, she began to walk faster.

Billy backed the tractor trailer up to the large hole in the ground as he gathered his shovel and began to pitch hog shit into the hole. The more he smelled the shit, the more upset he became at the stink on his cock. Stopping to look at the sunrise from the hilltop, he felt a hand on his shoulder. Billy turned to see Martha smiling at him, but her eyes showed concern. Billy said, "What do you want?"

Martha said, "I tried to stop you, and I am so sorry I could not."

"What the hell is wrong with you?" Billy growled as he stepped back.

Martha said, "I don't know and have been afraid to go to the doctor out of embarrassment."

"Is this a disease?" Billy shouted as he stepped back.

Martha said, "God, no; it's just a condition, but I will get it tested."

Billy said, "I am going to tell my parents." He dropped the shovel and began to walk toward the house. Martha grabbed Billy by the shoulders and tried to stop him, begging, "Please!" as she held on. Billy turned to push Martha away as she tripped over the shovel and fell into the deep hole. Billy turned and screamed as Martha disappeared into the darkness.

Billy ran down the hill, screaming for his father as he entered the home. Mr. Walton, after hearing the story, called David, their deputy cousin, to help. David arrived as the family sat on the porch.

"I need to talk to Billy alone," David said as he got out of the cruiser. Billy got up from the bench and walked with David up the hill, explaining the whole story. David smiled at Billy and said, "No worries. I will handle this. Someday, Billy, this farm will be yours, and if I do this for you, that means you owe me. Understood?" Billy nodded and began to cry. Deputy Walton said, "OK now, where is this bitch's car? Let us fix this. Billy, I want you to take the tractor and pull the vehicle into the barn. I will talk to your mom and dad." The deputy walked down the hill as Billy drove the tractor toward the woods and the car. Billy shook his head as he drove, thinking that the sinkhole got a name, and "Martha" suited it exactly right.

"Mr. Walton?" a voice spoke as Billy sat in class daydreaming and smiling.

"Yes, Mrs. Jones?" Billy replied to his new English teacher as she inquired about his assignment.

SNARES, SEDUCTION AND OTIS

Ricky left the lunch line and found Tim sitting in the back of the lunchroom alone. Ricky sat as Tim looked out the window, twisting his fork around into a pile of spaghetti. Finally, Ricky said, "Hey Stove Top, what are you doing sitting here with all your friends?"

Tim looked at Ricky and said, "Yeah," as he stopped playing with his food and looked back out the window. He said, "I really don't want to be here today. My dad is in jail; my sister won't talk to me, and I am tired of the Fraley brothers."

Ricky smiled and said, "Are you still the fastest kid in the eighth grade?"

Tim said, "What does that have to do with anything?"

Ricky smiled again and said, "How do you feel about a little payback?"

Tim turned his attention from the window and answered, "I can be the fastest kid!"

Ricky nodded his head and said to Tim, "I have a plan to fix those two." He tapped Tim on the shoulder as he moved his head up and down, looking at the front of the lunchroom right at the Fraley brothers, who were looking for a table.

Tim said, "I don't know Ricky; if my dad finds out I did something to those two after what he is going through, I might get in real trouble."

"But," Ricky said, "this isn't about your dad or theirs; it's about what they did to you; now watch me set this up!" Ricky got up and interrupted the Fraley Brothers in their search for a table. "Hey, puss bags, it took two of you to beat my friend; how about a rematch, two on two?"

Justin Fraley laughed and said, "Look, little Ricky is sticking up for his girlfriend."

Ricky looked at Justin and said, "What's a matter—afraid of a fair fight?"

Justin looked at his brother and said, "OK, since your girlfriend didn't learn the first time, when and where?"

"How about the park right after school? We will be there!" Ricky said as he turned and walked away. Tim continued to watch him approach.

"What was that all about?" Tim asked as Ricky sat down in front of his food tray.

Ricky said, "You and I are going to fight those two after school at the park." Tim felt his anxiety rising and a lump forming in his throat, unable to speak to what he just heard. Ricky smiled and said, "Don't worry. I have this all worked out; you'll see."

Tim realized that the lunch period was shortening, looked at Ricky, and said, "I hope you are right," as he began eating his lunch.

―

Jane arrived at the shop after driving around and paused before she entered; she stared at the pig masks in the shop window and thought to herself what she would say to the clerk who fucked her. Images swirled in her mind, like a movie broken and out of sequence. Then finally deciding to enter the shop, she made her way past the racks of clothes and novelties to the counter. Jane looked in the mirror behind the counter and adjusted her hair before ringing the bell.

Jane was somewhat surprised when an older woman walked from behind a curtain to approach her at the counter. "May I help you?" the old woman said in her soft rasp of a voice.

Jane said, "I am looking for the clerk who waited on me the other day."

"You might be thinking of my nephew Abraham," the woman said. "He is off today."

Jane said, "When will he be back?"

The old woman shrugged and said, "Sometime." She walked to the back behind the curtain. Jane, frustrated and angry, left the store as the old woman watched from a gap between the curtain and the door frame. The old woman turned once she was satisfied that Jane was gone and looked at her nephew, who was sitting at a table eating. "You have had another looking for you!" She placed her hands on her hips, waiting for a response.

Abraham looked at her and said, "Yes, I know. I heard her from back here. She won't be the last one. I am sure about that!" He smiled and continued to eat.

The aunt said, "This is my shop, not a dating spot."

Abraham said," I don't date them, and neither does my brother; we have a little fun!"

The Aunt shook her head and said, "Well, no more fun here, please!" as she joined him at the table. Abraham looked up from his plate and nodded in agreement.

Jane arrived at the house where she encountered the two men only to find the door leading up to the room to be locked. Jane pounded on the door as she yelled. Maybe someone inside would open it. Jane tried the handle one more time before stepping back to look at the windows on the second floor. Finally, Jane gave up and began to walk to her car before something else caught her eye—the bar across the street and its oddly crafted name. The Right Stuff. Jane puzzled over the bar as she tried to recall if she had ever noticed it before. The list of things to do shortening with unfulfilled goals for the day, Jane decided to cross the street to the bar and maybe gather some information about the house's occupants. She had visited twice now and knew very little.

Jane opened the large wooden door with the small, framed window at the top over her head, thinking who could see clear up there. The bar was darkened as the door shut behind her, causing no attention from the patrons as they continued life tangled in their own distraction. Jane walked up to the bar and sat as the bartender approached and said, "What can I get for you, Miss?" Jane ordered a vodka rocks as she looked the bartender over with curiosity and studied the bar from one end to the other before her drink was served.

As she paid, Jane asked the bartender if he knew anything about the house across the street. "Yes," the bartender said as he raised his eyebrow. "I know that when I was in the back grabbing ice, I could see you banging on the door, and I thought to myself, whoever made you angry should be worried." Jane's face flushed with embarrassment, and she said, "Thank you," as she picked up her glass for a sip. Jane moved from the bar to a table by the window to watch the house. Jane continued to sip and watch as the door to the bar opened.

Jane waited until the door closed and turned her head to look over her shoulder. She followed the man that entered with her eyes as he sat at the bar and waited for the bartender. He was wearing nothing more than a T-shirt and jeans, and his feet were covered in large boots that fit his muscular build. His hair was buzzed to the skin, and the tattoo of an eagle on his left bicep caught her attention. Jane continued to watch the man as he talked with the bartender like they were friends.

Jane couldn't help her curiosity any longer and got up from the table, neglecting her interest in the house and taking her drink with her. Jane approached the two men talking and sat at the stool next to them. She looked at the man seated next to her and interrupted his conversation with the bartender. "Hi, I am Jane Stover," she said as she extended her hand for a handshake. Without even looking at her, the man shook her hand. He continued talking with the bartender without even a brief interruption. Jane took her hand back as the man's firm grip released. Jane continued to look at the man and cleared her throat, waiting for a proper introduction.

The man finally broke from his conversation when the bartender left to visit with another customer. "Are you a prostitute?" the man said as he looked at Jane.

Jane said, "Hell, no, I am a nurse. Thank you!"

The man looked Jane up and down from her skirt to her hair and said, "Well, you sure look like one, and I am not interested."

Jane frowned and repeated herself in a stern voice. "I just said I was a nurse; now, who the hell are you?"

The man, caught off guard by the direct response, said, "I am Allen, Allen Mercer. I get approached by hookers all the time, and I am just used to it, so I am sorry if I offended you."

Jane paused and said, "You never came back?"

Allen looked at her and said, "What?" and he seemed confused.

Jane explained with excitement like a mystery had been solved. "I know you, or at least I know your aunt; she was in the hospital after falling and told me how you used to hunt in the cornfields with the Winchester and one day you disappeared. I thought Margaret was just forgetful, but she insisted, and I felt she was telling the truth. Wait. Here you are. Now I'm confused."

Allen looked at Jane and smiled. "So, you met my Aunt Margaret, eh; she is a wonderful lady who raised me. My uncle, not so much. He was an evil man, and when she realized it, she lost her mind."

Jane said with confusion, "So where did you go?"

Allen straightened his smile and said, "I am a hunter now."

Jane was even more confused and said, "Hunter?"

Allen said, "Yes, a while ago. I traveled after I left the farm and ran across this Turkish guy with a lot of money, and we hunt things."

"What kind of things? Don't you mean, like, animals?"

Allen nodded and said, "Yeah, sure." Allen said, "My friend got caught trespassing and has been locked up in the sheriff's office for three days. They have court on Thursdays, and I will have to help him out of this one."

"You will let him sit in jail? If he has so much money, why don't you just bail him out?"

Allen looked at his beer and said, "It's not that easy."

"That must have been the man I met with my husband when I stopped in this morning."

Allen said, "Your husband is locked up in the jail too? What did he do?"

Jane said, "He beat a man for what his boys did to our son to teach a lesson."

"Why don't you bail him out?" Allen asked.

Jane said, "Because we don't have the money."

Allen shrugged and said, "Maybe I can give you some money."

Jane said, "What do I look like, a prostitute?" Allen paused, followed by a roar of laughter that caused the whole bar to focus on him. Jane smiled and said, "That settles that," as she finished her drink, got up, and walked out of the bar, waving as she left.

Allen and the bartender watched her leave, and the bartender said, "That is one hot married piece of pie!" Allen shrugged as he returned to his beer. Jane got into her car, looking one more time at the house before resting while she waited.

Tim sat at his desk and kept his eye on the clock as the end of the school day approached. The other students whispered in pairs to each other as the teacher continued writing the chalkboard lesson. Tim nudged Ricky, seated in front of him, and said, "What are they whispering about?"

Ricky turned and whispered back. "I told everyone we are going to fight, and it's all over the school." Tim felt uneasy at his desk as his anxiety returned, and feelings of the beating he took in the tunnel returned to him as he rubbed his side. The sounds of the chalk and whispers became amplified to him as he looked around the classroom.

He looked at the door, plotting an early escape to the restroom. But unfortunately, the clock was not on his side, and within two clicks at the second, the bell chimed, and the teacher passed her parting greeting as the classroom emptied out. Tim got up and looked at his teacher with distress. He walked out into the hallway to find Ricky waiting on him with a smile.

Tim looked at Ricky and said, "We just hide, and maybe everyone will just forget about it."

Ricky looked at him and said, "Stove Top, you don't want to miss this. I have something special for those jerks, and you will be glad we did this." Ricky motioned Tim to follow him as the two boys stopped at their lockers to drop off books before making their way to the exit.

The two boys walked out of the school and onto the playground. The two boys jogged across the crosswalk to the entrance to the park. The boys arrived, overlooking the park to see the tunnel where Tim was beaten and the horde of kids standing in front of it. Ricky looked at his watch and said, "We are on schedule," as he looked at Tim and said, "When I tell you to run, you follow me and run." He tried not to laugh. The two boys walked down the hill and into the center of the crowd.

The Fraley brothers were standing with their fists clenched, ready to fight. Ricky looked at them and said, "Hold on!" as Susie walked up to Tim. Susie grabbed Tim by the hand, and before he could react, she kissed him on the lips for all to see as the kids gasped and laughed. Ricky put his hand on Tim's shoulders; his wide eyes and pounding chest left him totally numb to his surroundings, but it was short-lived as Susie withdrew from the kiss and let go of his hand on her way back to the front of the crowd.

Tim looked at Ricky as he told the brothers, "See, we ain't queer, and you two ain't shit!" The brothers stepped in front of the boys, towering over them both, as Justin got ready to reply, but suddenly he got interrupted by Ricky's hard kick in the balls. He hollered at Tim, who was still in between a kiss and anxiety, "Run!" Tim followed Ricky, who ran as the circle opened, letting the two boys pass. Justin Fraley got up off the ground with his brother's help, and they follow behind the boys, getting tangled in the circle of students and stumbling as they went. The students chased the pursuit as Ricky and Tim led them to the woods at the park's corner. Tim and Ricky had a slight lead on the brothers as they entered the woods. Ricky talked in his winded voice, "Follow right behind me."

Tim followed Ricky as he slowed down, crossed a small creek bed, and went into a clearing, stepping on a series of stones that made a path leading up a hill into a thick row of trees. Ricky stopped running and turned to place his hand on Tim's chest to stop his progress. Tim turned as he stopped to see the brothers come up the hill. Ricky smiled as the leaves and ground revealed a series of snares; with a swooshing sound, they grabbed the brothers by the feet and turned them upside down. The brothers now hung by their feet, courtesy of two large oak trees and sturdy twine. Ricky began to laugh; the brothers' confidence turned to panic as they cried in helplessness.

The mob of children arrived and began to laugh at the Fraleys swinging and crying slightly overhead. Ricky looked at Tim and said, "I told you, Stove Top!" Before turning his attention to the brothers and the mob, Tim looked at the crowd, cheering and laughing as the brothers remained swinging upside down.

Tim felt sorry for the brothers and what his dad had done to theirs. Ricky hollered at the Fraleys as the crowd quieted, "Don't mess with a farm boy who knows how to hunt!" Ricky went behind the row of trees beyond Tim and returned with a bucket. He looked at Tim and said, "My dad helped me set this up last night for you and your family, Stove Top."

Tim asked, "What is that in the bucket?"

Ricky said, "It's a gift from our pig Otis with a bit of water to make it really good." The smell was strong enough to make Tim almost sick as he turned pale. Ricky ran with the bucket before swinging, then stopping suddenly, and splashing the contents all over both brothers. The crowd erupted in more cheers as the brothers cried louder. They began to vomit from the smell and what ended up in their mouth. Ricky told the crowd, "Mess with Stove Top or any of my friends, and this is what you get!" Mr.

Clark appeared from behind the tree line and told the crowd it was time to go home.

The crowd began to scatter, leaving Susie as one of the last to go as she blew a kiss to Tim before walking with her friends back toward the open park field. Mr. Clark looked at the two brothers hanging, smelling like shit, coughing, and crying as they swayed from the twine.

"Now, listen, I hope you two boys have learned something today, and now you have a choice to remain here hanging until you figure out how to get free, or I cut you down, and you never bother these boys again!"

Justin Fraley said, "Please, we are sorry. Let us down."

Mr. Clark looked at Tim and Ricky, "You boys accept that apology?"

Tim spoke up first and said, "They have been through enough; we all have. Please get them down."

Ricky, puzzled by Tim's concerned tone, shrugged, and said, "Yeah, Dad, let them down." Mr. Clark pulled out his knife and cut both boys down as they quickly got to their feet and ran the creek bed until they were out of sight.

Mr. Clark turned to the boys and said to Tim, "I am sorry about what happened to you and your dad, but don't worry. I think that is the last time you will have to deal with them." Mr. Clark pointed at the trees and said, "My truck is just over there; grab the shit bucket, Ricky, and let's go. I will take you home, Tim."

Tim looked at Mr. Clark and Ricky and said, "No, that's OK. I want to walk. It will give me some space to think." Mr. Clark nodded, and Ricky turned and walked through the tree line.

Mr. Clark said, "Be careful going home, and if you need anything, let me know, and don't worry about Ricky; he has got his mom's temper and my resolve. He thinks of you as a brother and was only trying to help."

"I know," Tim said, "it has just been a lot for me this week." Mr. Clark nodded as he turned and walked into the tree line to follow Ricky. Tim walked down the hill before launching into a sprint across the open field.

Tim stopped before the tunnel and felt his anxiety had been erased. With a smile he walked into the tunnel without fear. Tim's thought shifted to his dad as the last piece to put his family back on track remained out of reach. He sighed out of missing his dad and wished he was close to his dad, like how Ricky and his dad were close. Tim imagined what it would be like to be Ricky's brother and have Mr. Clark as his dad. The thoughts occupied his mind as the end of the tunnel approached.

Tim's mind cleared as he got startled by Susie appearing from the walkway.

"Hey, Tim," she said as she backed him into the tunnel. Tim ended up against the tunnel wall as Susie kissed his lips and put her arms around him. Tim kissed Susie on the forehead and smiled as he looked at her. Susie took her hand and rubbed Tim's pants, causing him to get aroused. Susie looked up at Tim's eyes and said, "You want to walk back in the tunnel with me for a bit?"

Tim's face turned red with embarrassment as he had never experienced this before. He shuddered as he told Susie, "I have to get home." He moved from the wall and her arms and ran out of the tunnel toward home.

Susie sighed and said to herself, "Maybe next time." Tim, shocked by what just happened, realized as he ran what he just left behind, shaking his head, and hoping he didn't ruin her feelings for him.

CLAUDE FRALEY AND MISS JULY

The Fraley brothers remained silent as they walked in defeat along the river toward home. Finally, Justin said to Bobby, "We have to tell Dad what happened. How else will we explain being late and covered in shit?"

His brother remained silent and followed him and then finally said, "Dad is going to be so mad at us!"

Justin frowned as they walked and said, "What else is new?" Finally, the two brothers rounded the corner and walked up the path to the shack. The boys paused before turning the knob and entering from the porch.

Claude Fraley sat in his rocker in the center of the small living room littered with metal scrap and trash. He looked at the brothers with his swollen face and said, "What the fuck happened?"

Justin spoke up and said, "Supposed to get into a fight with Stover, but Ricky Clark and his dad had a trap waiting for us."

"Yeah, Dad!" the brother spoke up. "They snared us upside down and covered us in pig crap."

Claude said, "You leave those boys alone!" as he rocked into the light, exposing his face. "Look what happened to my face because of you two. Now, look at you, two idiots. I should have begged your mom to take you when she left. Now, you two need to grab some change and go to the car wash to rinse each other off. That change was to go for food; now we won't be able to eat! How am I going to have money for my beer? You boys go now. Get cleaned up, and when you come back, you will get punished. Right now, I can't stand that damn smell."

Justin grabbed some change from a small stand in the corner and nudged his brother's arm as the two boys hurried to leave the shack. Claude rocked back in his chair and grabbed his bottle of beer from the floor before realizing it was empty and threw it against the wall in anger, shattering the bottle into pieces and adding to the trash in the room.

Allen Mercer walked carefully through the woods as the sun faded into twilight. The cold night air and the glow of the moon made for the perfect night to hunt. Allen walked ever deeper into the woods, kneeling to check for animal tracks along the trail while holding his rifle in a sling close by his side. Finally, Allen paused at the top of a rise where the hill ahead of him sloped sharply, leading to a dim glow of a fire burning in the night at its bottom. As Allen watched, he noticed a series of various figures standing around the flames. Allen removed his sling from his back, pulling his rifle and scope to get a closer look. The strangers fed the fire to increase the light as Allen sat in the shadows watching, debating who he would shoot first.

The circle opened as another figure joined the group. Allen slowly took a position down on one knee as he leaned against a tall oak to steady himself and looked through the infrared scope again. The circle opened, and another joined, followed by grunting noise. Allen took aim at the last one that joined the group as he laid his fingertip across the trigger. The previous one removed his hood to reveal a pig mask on his head. The grunt continued as the complete removal of clothing continued.

Allen watched as the now naked man in the mask stepped into the circle closer to the fire. His infrared became distorted from the flames as he removed his eye from the scope, trying to see what was happening with both eyes. Allen decided to slowly move down the hill to get a closer look. He made it behind the next tree, only a few feet from where he was, and placed his back against the tree as he squared up and turned his head back toward the fire and the group. Allen heard sticks breaking and leaves rustling beyond his right shoulder down the slope.

He turned his head away from the fire and raised his scope to see. A bright flash blinded his eye illuminating the area, followed by a voice over a bullhorn. "This is Ohio Special Investigator Martin Donnell. You are under arrest for cult activity and trespassing on private property. Stay where you are!" Allen watched while a whole circle of law enforcement below him closed in on the fire. His first thought was to join the ring, but another in jail would not help his hunt. Allen slowly made his way back up the hill, away from the siege. As law enforcement closed, the suspects threw leaves in the fire, causing smoke to cover the slope and the gathering.

The officers choked on the burning leaves and became lost in the attempt. Finally, Martin stepped back on the hill and radioed Walton, Davis, and Mills, parked in a perimeter around the woods. "We got smoked out here!" Martin said over the radio. "Keep your eyes open; anyone makes it out, detain them." The officers arrived at the bottom of the hill only to find each other through the clearing smoke. Martin made his way down the slope and kicked the smoldering fire. "Team, this is now a crime scene; let's rope it off and hope the sheriff and his boys catch someone trying to leave these woods."

Allen reached the end of the woods and scoped the empty field. Allen saw the deputies parked alongside the road. He decided to sneak along the wood line in the opposite direction and into the cornfield.

Donnell rounded up his team after the area was secured, and no arrests were completed. "We came up empty here; let's head back to the motel and return in the morning when we have daylight to work with."

The Fraley brothers woke up in their small room, fighting off the cold, as they searched in a bit of a pile for clothes they shared. They worked to strip themselves of the still damp clothes from the car wash visit, and both settled for a pair of bibs and flannel bottoms underneath with red flannel shirts over the top. The boys grabbed a handful of biscuits from the stove as they passed their father resting in the rocker by the barrel stove. Claude woke up long enough to remind the boys to not cause any more trouble as they walked out of the shack and closed the door.

Claude got up and watched the boys through the window as they walked up beyond the yard and out of sight. Claude went into the kitchen and grabbed a bottle of whiskey from behind a brown cloth underneath the basin. Claude walked out of the shack's back door and across a narrow dirt path leading to an outhouse. Claude opened the door and placed his bottle down on the floor as he shut the door. Snapping his bibs loose, he peeled them past his belly to his ankles and sat on the seat.

Claude reached for a wobbly board on the wall, removing it to expose a magazine curled up between slats. Claude grabbed the whiskey bottle and took a drink, setting it beside him, then straightened out the magazine. "Miss July!" Claude smiled as he opened the magazine, "We have missed you!" Claude scooted on the seat and farted and got excited with every photo of July. Claude leaned back against the wall and reached for his cock under his belly as he stared at Miss July.

Claude stopped as he heard a noise from outside. Claude stood up and scooted around with his bibs still around his ankles as he cracked the door a bit to see. Claude pulled up his straps and snapped them and turned around to open the door to the outhouse. Claude pushed the door open and was met by a large man. The man drove Claude back into the shed, clutching him by the throat as Claude struggled; the man pushed down on Claude and slowly turned him headfirst toward the seat.

The prominent figure smiled, exposing his black eyes and razor-sharp teeth. The figure bit Claude on the neck, spraying bloodshot all over the inside of the outhouse. Claude stopped gasping as the life left his body. The monster smiled before biting out more flesh. He finished having his fill of meat, turned, and walked away.

Martin Donnell and his team joined Sheriff Davis and his deputies at last night's events. Donnell told everyone to look for any clue they could find. He looked at Davis, Mills, and Walton and said, "I don't understand how they escaped?" as he walked around the fire. "This scene is nothing like the last one. Where is the connection? We have no symbols or writing, no animal sacrifice, just this fire?"

Davis spoke up and said, "Maybe we interrupted them before they could get to that point?"

Donnell stopped and walked to the center of the scene and grabbed his bullhorn. "Attention, everyone. I need some of you to stay here, some of you to go to site A at the hilltop, and the rest of you to come with me over to the pit."

Donnell looked at the sheriff group and said, "I want you to go with me to the hole." On the bullhorn again, Donnell said, "We will collect all the evidence we can and return to the sheriff's office for a discovery meeting." Donnell headed up the hill with the sheriff group right behind.

Tim sat outside the school on the steps, watching the kids filter in, as he noticed the whispers. The passing students looked at him as they walked by. Tim saw the Fraley brothers and stood up, deciding to approach them. The brothers stopped as Tim stood between them and the school, and he said, "I am sorry for yesterday and everything that has happened. Can we please put all of this behind us?"

Justin Fraley looked at his brother, and both boys nodded and said, "We are sorry too!" Tim moved aside and let the brothers pass as Ricky approached with a confused look on his face.

"Tim, what did they want, a rematch?" Ricky asked as he smiled.

Tim said, "No, we apologized to each other now; it's over!"

Ricky shrugged and said, "OK, Stove Top, now what about Susie and that kiss? Are you ready for that rematch?" Tim smiled as the two boys turned and walked into the school.

Donnell, Davis, and the deputies arrived at the pit. Donnell dropped a rope in front of an oak tree that stood alone at the hill; he told the deputies to tie the rope around the tree while he took the other end of the line and tied it tight around his waist. "Now I want all of you to let slack out slowly to get into the pit and lower me. This rope is precisely one hundred feet; if I don't get to the bottom, then at least I can look around and hopefully get some clues."

Donnell places a headband with a searchlight on his forehead begins to back up as the deputies, and the sheriff slowly let slack out. It didn't take long before Donnell was in the hole and slowly descending. The den opened into what appeared to be a deep cave rather than a sinkhole shaft. The cool air in the cave came with the smell of death. Donnell hollered to the team above, "Something smells really bad down here!" *There must have been some recent dumping*, he thought to himself as he tried to look downward to see if he could find the source of the smell.

The light didn't reveal the cave floor, but Donnell could see several large holes in the cave walls before running out of rope. The smell became more vigorous, and Donnell realized there was no way to find the source and no longer tolerated the line digging into his back. The sheriffs team began to pull Donnell up as he made his request. The men pulled until Donnell was out of the hole, and the sheriff could help him to his feet.

"I couldn't find the bottom," Donnell said, "but the smell is horrible as if something was dumped and has begun to rot."

Mills and Walton looked at each other, and Walton said, "I don't think Billy has been dropping here lately, but maybe a wild animal fell in the pit."

Donnell said, "I saw several openings at the level I was and think there could be other entrance locations to the caving and, maybe, some that go to the bottom?"

Allen Mercer woke upon and old couch and looked around the old cabin and the new day through the window. Tired from the long walk last night and angry for coming up empty-handed, he walked to the fireplace to throw a few logs on before he turned and looked at his board on the wall containing a large county map with markings and writing that Allen had completed. Allen smiled and said, "You were right!" as he marked the spot with his finger. "Next time, I will get you and put all of this to an end."

BASEBALL IS NOT FOR EVERYONE

Allen sat down in a chair by the fireplace and looked at the map, lost in thought. Allen closed his eyes as his memories flooded the mind's eye. Tap, then tap was the sound against the wall as he pressed his hand against the wall, keeping the rhythm of passing the time. Settled in the bottom of a closet in a cut-down cardboard box with one blanket covered and wrapped around him, Allen laid in complete darkness. He stopped his tap to listen for noise beyond the door. Occasionally he would hear laughter followed by the squeaking of old bedsprings and footsteps shuffling out of the adjoining room. Allen wanted to be on the street, surrounded by people at a baseball game and smell the food under the lights. He was here in this closet, waiting and tapping. Finally, the door opened, and a voice called, "Come out and help me." It was the tired voice of his mother, who sat herself on the edge of the bed, only clothed in a loose-fitting slip.

As he came out and adjusted his eyes to the dim light, his mom pointed toward a bucket in the room's corner. Allen grabbed the bucket and carried it over to her as she pulled the slip over the bucket and straddled it to piss. Then, climbing back onto the bed, she instructed Allen to dump the bucket. Allen carried the bucket to the window. Opening the window, he placed the bucket onto the fire escape and climbed out to boost the bucket over the edge and dump it into the alley far below before taking the bucket back inside and placing it back in the corner.

His mother took a washcloth, placed it under her slip and between her legs, curled up on the bed, pulled money from under the mattress, and counted it. Allen stood and watched, waiting for an acknowledgment. "Come here, Allen!" his mother said as she moved over, placing her money back under the mattress.

Allen laid down close beside her as she draped her arm over him and began to whisper, "Close your eyes, and I will tell you a story. When I was a young girl, not much older than you are now, I lived by the ocean in a small village where I spent my days playing in the green fields overlooking the cliffs. My mom and dad were poor and wanted me to have a better life, so they sent me with my aunt and uncle on a ship here to America. My uncle had a trade business and had his own fleet of boats and trucks. I became a citizen and came to live here in Chicago in a lovely home. My aunt and uncle took good care of me and made sure that I had the best of everything. I was happy for several years, surrounded by friends and family, until things fell apart. My uncle lost his money along with everyone else, and we ended up living in the park. My aunt got sick and died; my uncle left me alone, heading west to look for work. I was on the streets and did what I had done to survive. I had you, and that is the only thing worth holding on to, and this is not much but, this is all we have. So, rest my son, and tomorrow may bring us luck."

Allen never made it that far as he was already asleep in his mother's arms. The following day Allen awoke to the sound of a door creaking closed. He looked up to see his mother freshly dressed, returning from the washroom down the hall. She smiled at Allen as he rubbed his eyes and told him to grab his clothes and get washed up. Allen went to the trunk, grabbed some clothes from his side, and hurried down the hall to wash up. He emerged moments later, dressed, and smiling as his mother waited for him in the hallway.

Down the many flights of stairs, they went—and into the bustle of the Chicago day. "Alley," his mom said as she nodded and smiled in delight at the nickname, she gave him before grabbing him by the arm, "You know where we are going today?" Allen looked up and paused in silence, unsure of the answer. "We are going out to Wrigley for some ball!" Allen smiled with excitement as she led him down the street and to the bus stop. Waiting with nervousness, Allen watched down the road for the bus to arrive. Time seemed to stop, and the bus seemed like it would never succeed as Allen took his eyes off the approaching traffic only to look at his mom and smile. Finally, the bus arrived, and they boarded it to head to the stadium. Allen watched the streets and all the people as the bus made its way through the city. The road came to a large lot where the bus stopped, and Allen hurried out the door, waiting for his mother to follow.

They followed the flow of people through the gates and into the stadium.

Allen found a seat for them right behind the home plate. Excitement and the smell of popcorn filled the air. Allen tried to explain baseball to his mother as the game began, but he paused when his mother began moaning. Her eyes fluttered and swirled, and the crowd started roaring and cheering the louder she groaned. Allen's seat began bouncing rapidly up and down and making a knocking noise. Allen looked around as everyone looked at him and cheered louder and louder; his mom began laying on her side and groaning. Just then, everything went black, and Allen sat up. He was awake in his box in the darkness of the closet. No bed resting with Mom, no baseball. Allen began to tear up with disappointment as his mom entertained a man in the next room. Wiping away the tears, Allen lay back down in his box and covered up with the blanket over his head to muffle it.

Then, drifting in and out of sleep, Allen was brought to consciousness by his mother calling. Allen crawled out of the box to find his mom sitting on the edge of the bed, counting money. Feeling this familiar feeling, Allen grabbed the bucket from the corner of the room and carried it over to her. She tucked the money under the mattress and straddled over the bucket, grabbing the washcloth, and washing. She placed the washcloth down, and Allen grabbed the bucket as she climbed back into bed. He took the pail to the fire escape out the window and dumped it into the alley below. Coming back inside, he placed the bucket in the corner and went to the closet door to get back to sleep. His momma asked him, "Why don't you come to lie with me?" and Allen screamed, "It's because I hate you!" His mom paused and said, "The hell with you then! I didn't want you but couldn't get rid of you, and I do the best possible!" Before the argument could finish, a knock at the door came. Allen went into the closet, shut the door, crawled back into the box, and lay down.

His mother opened the door to greet the man on the other side. She went back to the bed and pulled up her slip, exposing her pussy. She told the man, "Ten dollars, and you can have me." The man walked into the dimly lit room and stood to look at her for a moment. His hair and shirt were dripping, soaked almost entirely.

He lowered his brow and stared at her offer and said, "You know, it's funny. I have been walking the alley outside from work for five years. I spend all day down at the bar bouncing wrong customers out the door. I have been spat on and fought, burned with a cigar, and really pushed. I choose the alley because it's quiet, and no one would ever try and mug me after work because they would not live. We crossed paths tonight because of you. You ruined my quiet by dumping cum and water on me, and whatever stink came out of that proud little pussy. I am not here to fuck you; I decided that when I walked up the stairs and stood outside your door. I am here to kill you just for being the disgusting whore that you are!"

Before she could react, the large wet man was on top of her with his hands squeezing her neck. Inside the closet, Allen turned and covered his ears, assuming his mother's activities' usual routine. She moaned as usual, but then quickly, there was silence, followed by a door slamming. Allen waited for his mother's call, and it did not come. Allen remembered the last time he opened the door without a mother's request and will never forget what he saw. Allen slowly stood up and opened the door ever so slightly if he needed to close it in a hurry.

He could see a dim light through the crack and his mother lying on her side with her face turned away from him. Allen opened the door, went to his mother, and tugged on the strap of her slip, waiting on her to roll over. Allen placed his hand on her shoulder and took it away when it felt strange with her not responding. She felt as if she had become so still that even her skin felt inflexible to the touch, like his leather belt from his beautiful clothes. Allen climbed on the bed to peek at his mother's face, seeing if she was sleeping, and that is when he saw a look he would not soon forget. It was dead with her eyes and mouth open and tongue hanging out. Allen jumped off the bed and ran down the hall, banging on every door and screaming for help.

He could recall when he first arrived on that warm summer day, and his uncle took his hand as he led him to the porch to meet his waiting aunt. Allen could recall the feeling around the dinner table with his new parents. As he remembered when he was older, the pain soon followed, and he first noticed his uncle at the cornfield edge, talking to someone hidden between the leafy green rows. The look in his uncle's eyes as his uncle saw him watching was the same look, he gave the pigs as he loaded them onto his truck and drove them to slaughter.

Then there was the last day. The day he was a man, and for his birthday, his uncle walked him to the field as the brown rows of corn shook in the wind. The day his uncle stopped him halfway from the house and the field and said, "This is not for you, son, and I am sorry," before walking into the area, hollering with his hands raised high, "Take me instead!" The day his uncle disappeared.

Allen opened his eyes and looked at the dying fire before getting up, throwing on his coat, grabbing his rifle, and walking out of the cabin as the day folded into the evening.

HOW THEY ALL UNRAVEL

The Fraley boys walked the river home, skipping stones and throwing sticks into the muddy water. The brothers walked up the hill with the shack in sight. Justin opened the front door, entering the hut followed by his brother. It was noticeably quiet with their dad absent from his chair and the fire out. Justin looked out the back door and noticed that the outhouse door was slightly open. The boys walked out together and knocked on the door with no reply. The boys opened the door to find the outhouse was bloody and empty. Figures surrounded the boys; they tried to fight past the strangers but were overcome by the evil that happened next as the screams carried outside the shack and echoed to the river.

The morning arrived at the courthouse as Thomas waited his turn before the judge. The judge called Thomas Stover to the front bench as the clerk read charges for the judge. Thomas looked over at the sheriff, who was standing to the left of the judge. The judge looked at Thomas and said, "We have assault with a crowbar?"

Thomas replied, "Yes, sir."

The judge said, "tell me. What the hell were you thinking?"

Thomas answered and said, "I wasn't!"

The judge said, "I see where you served in Nam?"

Thomas nodded and said, "Yes, your honor."

The judge said, "Terrible mess over there; I lost my nephew." The judge looked at the sheriff and said, "Where is Mr. Fraley?"

The sheriff replied, "He doesn't appear to be present, your honor."

The judge said, "Well, then how am I supposed to see for myself what these charges are?" The judge looked at Thomas and said, "Today is your lucky day. Case dismissed!" The bailiff called the next case as Thomas left the courtroom escorted by the sheriff.

Thomas passed Ayaz and nodded, saying good luck as he passed Allen Mercer, who was seated on the bench behind Ayaz. Allen Mercer had a stern look on his face that caused Thomas to turn away and look at the sheriff as they headed out the double doors. "Do you know that guy back there?" Thomas asked the sheriff, as they walked down the hall.

Sheriff Davis paused and said, "Yes. That is Allen Mercer. Last I knew he lived at his family farm west on ninety-two." Thomas thought to himself, *I wonder how he knows Ayaz?* The sheriff and Thomas left the small courthouse. The sheriff said, "Thank you for cooperating, and I told you this would all work out."

Thomas shrugged and said, "Now what?"

The sheriff replied, "Let's get you back to the station so you can change out of that jumpsuit, and I will drop you off at your truck as promised."

Thomas looked at the sheriff and said, "What about Fraley?"

The sheriff looked at Thomas and said, "I will have to inform him the charges dropped because he failed to appear. That means you stay away from old Claude and forget all about this. Understood?" Thomas nodded as the two men got in the car and drove off.

FERTILE DIRT STUDIO

Tim entered the empty house and sat relaxed on the couch. Tim walked up the stairs to his room and closed the door. He decided to lay on his bed and closed his eyes for a moment as he rested his head on the pillow. Tim got up, grabbing a pack of cigarettes from the stash in the floor, removing one cigarette, then pausing to remove another to place it in his ear. He returned the pack to the floor and left his room. He walked down the hall and looked out at the roof over the back porch.

Opening the window, he slid out onto the top and sat with his back against the corner; he lit up and inhaled, watching the smoke drift away in the air and looking around with each puff. He finished his last drag and leaned forward to drop the butt into the gutter. Tim turned and climbed back in the window. Tim walked back down the hall and turned to walk into his room only to find his father sitting on the bed, staring down at the floor. Tim paused as he realized he forgot to place the board back. Then, calmly, and casually, Tim spoke. "Hey, Dad, I didn't hear you come home."

Thomas turned his gaze from the floor directly into Tim's eyes and said, "Son, you have been caught, and there is no need to pretend otherwise." Tim's eyes widened as he felt his throat dry; he tried to speak but realized it would not be a good idea. Tim nodded and looked at the floor as the cigarette fell from his ear. Thomas picked up the smoke and stood up. "A man owns up to his mistakes, Tim, and I will help you understand this. Tell me where you got this." Thomas held out the cigarette in front of Tim's face.

Tim walked to the stash in the floor, picked out the rest of the packs, and handed them off to his father. Thomas grabbed the boxes, threw them on the bed, and grabbed Tim by the back of his head while forcing the cigarette into his mouth as he instructed Tim to chew. Thomas asked Tim again who gave him the cigarettes. Tim began to gag on the paper and tobacco. He began to cry, and he felt his stomach tighten and nausea begin to take root. Thomas let go as Tim fell to his knees and vomited on the floor, followed by gasping for breath and spitting. Thomas repeated himself, "Where did these come from?" as Tim began to calm down.

Tim, not wanting to get Molly into the middle, said, "Ricky, it was Ricky!"

Thomas shook his head in disgust and mumbled, "I will sort this out with Clark. Stay away from Ricky, and you are grounded!" Thomas left Tim's room and headed down the hall, stomping with every step as Tim looked at the vomit-covered floor and rubbed his forehead to try and ease his newly formed headache. He could hear his father on the phone with Mr. Clark and the one-sided conversation loaded with anger and a lot of fucks.

Tim thought to himself as he stood up, I hope I die before going to school tomorrow.

Molly approached the house, passing her dad's truck in the drive, and hesitated to step on the porch when she heard her father yelling. She hoped that he did not find out about John because she knew how fierce his temper was and did not want to live in Indiana with her cousins as he had threatened before. Molly approached and decided to sit in the swing. She opened her literature book and flipped a page to *Romeo and Juliet* and began reading. She was not through the introduction before the front door opened, and her father stepped out on the porch, clinching his fist, and looking in the driveway. "Have you seen Mom?" he said without even looking at Molly.

Molly turned and stood up to show respect and said, "No, I just got home?" almost to say she was clueless about his anger.

Thomas turned to Molly and said, "Did you know about this?" as he pulled a cigarette out of his work shirt pocket.

Molly intuitively said, "Where did that come from?" as she instantly knew her brother got caught. Thomas nodded and sighed as he shut the door, got into his truck, and left without saying any more.

Molly went into the house, calling out for Tim as she walked through the living room. Tim softly said, "Up here!" as she approached the stairs. She ran up the stairs and turned into Tim's room to see him cleaning the floor with a mop and a bucket. Tim stopped, pulled his hair from his face, looked at Molly, and began to cry as he talked. "I got caught," he sniffled. "And Dad made me eat them!" Molly frowned in pity as Tim proceeded to tell her that he didn't tell him it was Molly who had been supplying. Molly went in for a hug, and Tim turned and said, "I am covered in puke and grounded, and Ricky will never speak with me after what Dad said to Mr. Clark. I don't want to hug; I want to clean up and die! Molly, you will be gone soon, and I will be with Dad and his rules and Mom, who is always gone! Where is Mom?" Tim paused as he looked at Molly.

Molly shrugged her shoulder and said, "She probably got called into work."

Tim finished his cleanup and walked out of his room, carrying a mop and bucket of puke water, and ending his conversation with Molly as he walked down the stairs. "I am going to shower and then die!" Molly shook her head and walked downstairs after Tim, turning to walk back out to the porch and sit on the swing.

Sheriff Davis made his way to the Fraley home, parking at the lane's start beyond the trees and scattered junk. The sheriff walked, arriving at the porch shack, knocking at the door, and peeking in the windows. The sheriff decided to walk around the back of the shack. The sheriff looked around the corner of the cabin and noticed the outhouse door flapping in the wind and banging as it hit the outhouse frame. The sheriff drew his pistol as he slowly approached the outhouse, cocking the hammer. Davis grabbed the door as it swung in the wind, opening it wide to reveal an empty stall.

The sheriff noticed the blood splattered inside the stall as he bent down to pick up the magazine curled up on the ground. Davis uncocked his pistol, returning it to his holster and throwing the magazine in the outhouse before turning his attention to the shack. The sheriff walked to the back door of the shack and turned the knob. Davis walked into the quiet shack from a dark room to a dark room to find nothing and no one. The sheriff walked back around to his car, grabbing the radio as he sat, and called Martin Donnell. "Martin, this is Sheriff Davis; we have another crime scene. Meet me on old road thirty-six before the river. You will see my car."

Martin replied and said, "On my way."

Jane began to second guess her thoughts after several visits. What would she do if she caught up with the two men in masks? What would she say? Now that she couldn't get the images and the feelings of pleasure out of her mind, was she here to confront them or get dominated by them again? Jane finally cleared her mind and decided to go to work as she backed her wagon and headed down the street toward the hospital.

Thomas drove past the hospital looking for the station wagon on his way out of town to his favorite hangout, the Damp's Bar. Walking in, he went to his usual stool, far away from the crowd and the congestion. Pulling up a bowl of peanuts, he motioned for a beer from Mack, the bartender. Mack dropped off the draft, foaming at the head, and scooped up the quarter left by Thomas. Thomas watched the people as he kept his focus on the TV above the bar. The beer made the crowd less noticeable and the news a whole lot funnier. Thomas imagined himself as a news anchor with the perfect life in the ideal town with an obedient, easily correctable son.

To have an exemplary life like that would be great. The quarters fell as the drafts flowed, and Thomas frequented the restroom in the back and staggered back. The last round was when Thomas could no longer piss in the urinal and sprayed his boots. Leaning up against the wall, he wiped off the piss with a paper towel as best he could and walked out of the almost empty bar into the cold night air. Across the lot, he slid into his truck and decided to sit to gain his bearing.

His head felt heavy, and before he realized it, he was lying down on the seat asleep. It was a shout that shattered his slumber as Thomas awoke from his place, wiping the drool from his mouth and sitting up in the darkness to see his vehicle, one of few in the back of the stone lot beside an old garage where he usually parks. Thomas brushed his hair back with his hand and looked around for the source of the shout. Then he saw a flicker of movement behind the bar underneath a security light. Thomas got out of the truck and ducked behind the fender. While softly closing the door, he kept both eyes fixed on the bar. Another scream rang out just at the edge of darkness, out of view. Thomas ran to the back corner of the building, ducked, and turned to look straight down the back wall. Still unable to see, he decided to make his way around the front to the opposite corner. Thomas, half ducking, ran around the building and crept up to the corner. He turned his eyes around the edge, looking right at the dumpster. Instead, he saw a woman struggling underneath a large man in the dim light from the alley. Without hesitation, Thomas ran while tightening his fist, grabbed the man by the back of the neck, and landed a punch right on the jaw. That was too much for Thomas as he stepped back, still dizzy from the hangover. The man stopped pinning the woman against the dumpster and turned to snarl at Thomas. The man was huge, and his eyes flickered in the light like two diamonds flashing in between the black. Thomas looked on the ground for anything to use as a weapon to help his situation. Just as the man approached, Thomas found a beer bottle and smashed it on the man's face, followed by a kick right in the nuts. The man hunched over as he fell to one knee, looking at the ground. Then he looked up at the woman with his bloody face, then turned to look at Thomas. His eyes flickering and skin shining white under the light, he turned to get up and ran down the alley into the darkness.

Thomas, relieved, went to his knees then sat directly on the gravel lot before calling out to the woman. "Hey, are you OK?" he asked as he caught his breath.

"I think he was trying to have his way with me and kill me. I saw him watching me from inside the bar, and he followed me out as I was walking home."

Thomas said, "Walking isn't safe," as he got up off the ground and brushed himself off.

She looked up at Tom, exposing her smooth skin and deep blue eyes in the light. "Do you remember me, Trixie?" she asked.

"I am the night shift dispatch at the sheriff's department. This is my normal night off; deputies usually cover me Thursday and Friday."

Thomas said, "We should call the police."

Trixie looked at him and said, "You hurt him. I will hate to see you get in trouble if they find him. Besides, I think he bit my neck or cut it!" She exposed her neck to Thomas from under her hair, showing two scratches on the skin.

"It looks like he scratched you," Thomas said, looking at her wound. "I think you will be OK," he said as she brushed her hair back over her neck.

Trixie kissed Thomas on the cheek and said, "Thank you," as she turned to walk away.

Thomas said, "Wait, where are you going? Don't you remember what just happened?" Trixie stopped and turned as Thomas pointed out his truck and said, "I could take you home."

Trixie looked down the street, then back at the ride before turning to look at Thomas and smiled. "Sure, if you don't mind." Thomas shrugged his shoulders and nodded. Finally, Thomas and Trixie arrived at her apartment building as Thomas stopped to let her out.

Trixie paused and asked Thomas if he wanted to come in for a cup of coffee. Thomas declined. Trixie said, "OK, how about you meet me back at the bar tomorrow night for a drink? Let's say seven, and you can take me home—maybe this time without rescuing me." Before Thomas could say anything, Trixie grabbed his thigh and kissed him on the cheek. Thomas cracked a smile and watched her walk away and into her building before leaving. Finally, Thomas made it home and felt excitement as he walked into the house. He walked down the hall, took off his clothes, and threw them in the basket in the bathroom before getting in the shower to get the beer and cigarette smell off him. He got out of the shower, grabbed his robe, and walked into his bedroom. Thomas took off his robe and crawled into bed and was asleep shortly.

It was a short night for Tim as yesterday's events left him still sick and upset about facing Ricky. Tim rolled out of bed, already dressed in his pajamas, and went downstairs to see if Mom was up. Jane was in the kitchen at the table wearing her uniform, working on paperwork, and sipping some coffee. Tim slowly walked into the kitchen, holding his stomach to inject theatrics into his nervous condition.

Jane looked up from her paperwork and said, "Morning, Timmy," as she noticed his condition. "What's wrong," she asked as Tim didn't even smile.

Tim started to explain by saying, "Dad—" but Thomas came around the corner, finishing his sentence before he could finish.

"Dad caught me smoking and punished me," Thomas said with a firm voice.

"What kind of punishment?" Jane asked as she looked directly at Thomas.

"I made him eat a cigarette, and he got sick. That's better than the ten boxes that I caught him with."

"Ten Boxes!" Jane replied, startled. "Where did you ever get that?"

Thomas answered again, "From that kid Ricky Clark!"

"Tom, please no more feeding our son tobacco."

"Don't worry, Janie. I called his father and grounded our son!"

Jane looked at Tim as he looked at the floor. "Tim, are you sick?" Tim nodded as he gagged a bit. Jane said, "Your father is right. Still, if you don't feel well, I don't want you going to school.

Stay home and take the weekend to get better." Tom looked at Jane, then sighed with frustration and walked out of the room on his way out the door. He was mumbling as he stepped.

"Now, Tim, I am leaving today for the Toledo conference, so watch TV, rest, or sleep, but be good until your dad gets home." Tim nodded, relieved, and walked upstairs, passing his sister as he went into his room. Molly walked down the stairs and into the kitchen, unassuming to her brother's fate. Jane said calmly, looking up from the table, "I am leaving today for Toledo. I need you to help your dad and look after Tim this weekend."

Molly smiled and said, "Sure, Mom, whatever you need!" as she went to hug her and walk out the kitchen door leading through the backyard and into the alley. As she turned to look back at the house, she saw Tim looking back at her through the upstairs window. Molly turned and continued her way to school.

Tim went to his bed and laid down to rest with the day clear to relax. Tim covered his head with his blanket and soon felt sleep grabbing at his consciousness as he drifted away. *It was quick*, he thought as his sister grabbed him by the shoulder. Tim felt rested and alert but paused before mentioning he was awake because of no dream. Tim turned and looked at Molly as she brushed back her hair with her fingers and shook her head as she said, "It is after four o'clock, and Dad will be home soon. I am going down to get dinner ready for Dad, so come and help, and maybe we can talk him into letting you get ungrounded." Molly left the room, and Tim could hear her as she walked downstairs, still talking to him about being ungrounded. Tim grabbed some clothes from his dresser, went into the bathroom, and got into the shower. Rinsing off quickly, he hurried through getting dressed and met Molly in the kitchen to help her with dinner. Molly looked at Tim and said, "Now, let's work together, and we can persuade Dad to let you go out with me tonight." Just as Molly said that the front door shut. They could both hear Thomas at the door before he walked into the kitchen to place his lunch box on the counter. He looked at his children and asked about dinner.

Before Molly could answer, Thomas looked at her and Tim and said, "Hold that thought. I was going to get a shower." Thomas half smiled, remembering Trixie, and walked out of the kitchen.

—

Dr. Brady and Jane arrived at the conference, checking into the hotel under separate rooms to keep undercover. Jane walked directly to her room and dropped her bags inside the door before stretching out on the bed, waiting for the doctor to finish the day's conference before joining her. Her body, still aching from the brutal fuck she received just more than a day ago, did nothing to diminish her desire for the doctor. Jane got up off the bed and went into the bathroom to get undressed, removing her clothes.

She returned to the bed and crawled under the sheet, leaving half her body exposed to reveal enough to interest the doctor. Jane turned on the TV and found interest in a vampire movie. Time passed, and Jane fell asleep as the vampire stalked his prey.

Dr. Brady finished his lecture for the day, dropped off his suit, and changed into leisure clothing before making his way across the hotel to Jane's room using the spare key; he looked around the hall as he entered. Finding her on the bed sleeping with the TV on, the doctor removed his shoes, unbuttoned his pants, and let his cock hang exposed. Then, climbing up to the bed, he rubbed Jane on the pussy as his cock began to harden. Jane awoke to find his cock near her face, grabbed it, and began to work her mouth around it. The doctor stopped massaging her, pulled off his shirt, threw it to the floor, and then backed up from Jane's reach, removing his pants on the floor placing it with the shirt.

The doctor stopped and said, "Fuck! What is this?"

Jane turned and said, "What? What is what?"

"This!" the doctor directed Jane to the mirror. Jane looked in the mirror and paused with shock. "This fucking star!" the doctor said. "Why is there a star tattooed on your ass?"

Jane looked at the mark, and it didn't resemble an ordinary star, and it cut into her like some animal marking with dried up blood and skin. Jane paused and then remembered that she noticed this in the mirror after being drugged and returning home. The doctor began to put his clothes back on as Jane turned and sat on the bed. "What are you doing?"

The doctor replied, "I will get my bag; we need to clean you up, and you need to tell me what happened."

Jane was clueless, could not remember how this exactly happened, and began to cry. What was she going to say to the doctor, or what would her husband say? Why did they mutilate her?

Thomas got up from the table, thanking Molly and Tim, who were still seated and eating. Before he left for the den, Molly looked at Tim and then said, "Dad, could Tim and I go to the drive-in tonight? It is the last one for the season." Thomas turned, looked at his children, and paused, followed by a clear and firm *no*. Molly shrugged and frowned as Tim stared at his mashed potatoes, not moving a muscle.

Finally, Thomas looked at Molly and said, "Tomorrow maybe, but not tonight. Mom is gone, and I have plans and am not sure what time I will be home. So, you need to watch your brother for me right here." Molly grumbled, and Thomas raised his voice in a growl. "I said, No!"

Molly whispered, "OK, Dad, I hate your stupid rules."

Thomas said, "OK, forget the weekend; you are both grounded," as he grabbed his jacket and walked out the door. Thomas got into his truck and drove away.

Molly watched from the kitchen window as Thomas went down the street, then turned to Tim and said, "How about it?"

Tim looked up from his plate and said, "What?"

Molly said, "Let's go to John's and get out of here!"

Tim looked at Molly with a nervous expression and said, "What about Dad? If he finds out, we are—"

Molly stopped him and said, "We are what? Grounded even more? We are a little too old for a spanking, and besides, when he comes back late from the bar, he won't remember anything, and we will already be home." Molly smiled and said, "Come on, Timmy, just for a few hours. I promise!"

Tim stood up and said, "This time I get to go to the drive-in for a bit and maybe see Susie?"

Molly laughed as she made kissing sounds and said, "OK, and we can meet halfway by the drive-in." Molly and Tim hurried through the dishes laughing and joking, pretending to be their father, and before too long, they went right out the back door down the alley and made their way toward the edge of town.

Jane waited on the bed, still lying on her stomach, waiting for the doctor to return. Finally, he arrived, came into the room, placed his bag down, drew up a shot, and stuck Jane right in the ass. Jane turned as she screamed a bit and said, "What the hell was that?"

The doctor said, "I picked up some penicillin at the local drug store and some things to clean this—whatever it is." The doctor asked Jane as he scrubbed, "What has caused this?"

Jane, who had time to come up with a lie and grew tired of the notion, told the doctor, "I got fucked and not by Thomas. I have a problem. I have always had a problem." Jane continued to confess as the doctor listened. "When I was a young girl about sixteen—I don't talk about this much, but this will explain—I used to ride my bicycle out along the countryside to the valley. There were many old barns and farms, and along the way, I used to play in them, and curiosity always led me to explore different places. That's when it happened. One day I went into this barn on the edge of this field, which led into a wooded forest; I can still feel the breeze from the woodland as I made my way to the barn. As I went through a place in the barn where the boards had split behind an old tractor, I heard the noise. It was a woman screaming, but it was different than any scream I had ever heard before." Intrigued, the doctor paused his work to listen as he sat with Jane on the bed.

Jane continued and closed her eyes to recount the images. "This young couple was on the floor of the barn, and she was on her knees, getting fucked hard; she was sliding around the blanket as he pulled her back where he wanted her. My first thought was to sneak out and go home, but the more I watched, the more interested I became. Finally, I moved closer to get a better look and realized that these were two that I knew from school, and they were only a few years older than I was. I am not sure who noticed me first, but they both began to shout after stopping. I turned and ran toward the exit, but I was grabbed by the boy while his cock was still hanging out of his pants. He looked at me in my dress and cowgirl boots and told me it would be OK as he brought me back to the blanket on the floor. I didn't know what was about to happen, but his girlfriend approached and grabbed me underneath my dress and pulled down my panties from the front, and before I could react, probably from nerves, I felt it. The boy was behind me, and he had pulled my dress up, exposing my ass with his cock pressed right against my cheeks. He placed his hand on the back of my neck and pushed forward, then it happened. He spat on his hand and rubbed my pussy, pulling me tight as he placed his cock inside me. It hurt like no pain I had ever felt, but that was brief. I fell to my knees with his second pump. I tried to get away, but on his third attempt, finally I stopped moving and began to enjoy it. He went faster and deeper as the other girl watched and smiled. He had taken my first time away forever, and I didn't care. I liked it; squeezing my hips and thrusting back and forth, I felt free and alive like I had never felt before. He liked it and fucked me hard until I felt his cum inside me, then he stopped. And I collapsed on the blanket with my ass in the air like I am now."

The doctor interrupted Jane. "What does that have to do with this mark?"

Jane said, "Everything." Jane continued to explain. "Was it rape? Most would think so. I was young and vulnerable, confused, and excited, but when I left there and walked my bicycle home and cleaned up, I realized I liked it, and I wanted more. I realized then I was an instant addict. That was the beginning of all of this," Jane said. "When I was seventeen, I was shipped off to live in Indiana with my aunt. She was a strict Catholic and raised me like a nun. My Aunt Betty lived on a small farm by herself and spent most of her time attending church. By my second month there, I was living at the church. At first, I was reluctant to confess to the young priest responsible for the church youth. But slowly, I shared my experiences and desires with him at confession. The first time I stepped in his box he was startled until I sucked his cock. The priest couldn't get enough of me. I spent the next two years fucking every altar boy that was old enough to cum, all from inside the confessional. Finally, the priest had a conscience crisis and left the church, and that is when I met Thomas. Thomas was more mature and working with his brother on church renovation. I convinced my aunt he was everything I wanted, and when I turned nineteen, we got married then moved back here. I was pregnant with Molly, a gift from young Father Stanley, and soon after, I had Tim. I was calm when Thomas left for Vietnam and waited for his return. I have been right all these years until you. Then the two guys fucked me harder than I could ever imagine; they drugged me and carved that star in my ass. I am a hypocrite. I preach to my kids to go to church and pray, but I can't control this. Thomas has changed ever since Vietnam; he seems so disconnected and angry. I have a craving that I can't fill."

The doctor looked at the star again and said, "I think someone knew this, that it's not an ordinary star. Someone marked your deeds; it's a pentagram."

"Pants what?" Jane was perplexed.

"It's the mark of evil."

Jane turned over and said, "Can you fix it?"

The doctor said, "I wouldn't know until it heals and scars."

Jane stared at the doctor and said, "I will pay for my sins sooner I think." Then she felt desire well up in her. "Come on, Doc! You patched me up. Now how about making me feel better?" She placed her hand on his leg and used her other hand to touch her pussy and her fingers to spread open her smooth lips, exposing her pink to the doctor.

Thomas arrived at the bar and sat in his truck a bit, thinking about his kids and Jane. Fearing he was about to do something wrong, Thomas restarted his vehicle and looked behind him but stopped when he saw Trixie staring at him through the driver's side mirror. Thomas paused and pulled the truck forward back into the parking spot before stepping out. He looked at Trixie with her short blond, red hair and even shorter skirt and said, "I was unsure about this. I am married."

Trixie smiled and said, "Oh yeah? Well, where is your wife now?" as she grabbed Thomas by the arm and led him in the bar.

Thomas headed for his usual spot before Trixie led him to a booth in the corner where the dim light from the pool table was the only light. The waitress came by and got the order of beer and dropped off some peanuts. Trixie said, "So where is your wife tonight?"

Thomas said, "A conference in Toledo." Thomas looked at Trixie and said, "What about you? Why is someone as attractive and young as you are hanging out in places like this?"

Trixie leaned forward and said in a soft voice, "I had spent my life moving around. I left home when I was a teenager and hoped for the day Mr. Right would cross my path. Are you Mr. Right?" Trixie asked as Thomas shuffled a bit in the booth.

Thomas said, "No, I am married," shaking his head."

Trixie looked at Thomas and sat back at the booth for a minute; she turned and looked back at Thomas and said, "That's sad that you say that." Thomas frowned and took a drink from his beer. Trixie proceeded to talk. "How about we be friends? I want to be the type of friend you don't tell your wife about." Thomas looked up from his beer and was speechless.

Finally, Thomas said with a lump in his throat, "Not sure I could do that."

Trixie smiled and said, "I would have to teach you how!"

Thomas looked around the bar, looked at Trixie, and said, "Do you want to get out of here?"

Trixie smiled and said, "Finish that beer, and let's go." Thomas chugged the last little bit as they got up, and they walked out the back door into the cold air of the night.

Thomas looked at Trixie as they got seated in his truck and said, "Now, where do we go?"

Trixie smiled as she pulled up her skirt, exposing her hairless pink slit, and said, "How about we go to my place?" Thomas felt a flush of excitement, forgetting everything he cautiously said in the bar, and proceeded to start the truck and drove into the alley just minutes from Trixie's place.

They pulled up to the curb, and before Thomas could even get stopped, Trixie sprung out of the passenger seat and right out the door, jumping on the sidewalk as Thomas stopped and looked. She pulled up her skirt again, this time exposing her ass to him. Thomas got out, walked around the truck, and scooped Trixie off her feet, carrying her to the apartment entrance. He let her down long enough for her to fetch her keys and open the door; walking in, Thomas kicked the door behind them shut and thrust her against the wall as he pulled his throbbing erection out of his pants and looked into Trixie's eyes while pushing inside of her. Grabbing her underneath her ass to hold her against the wall, Thomas continued to fuck her. He closed his eyes while she kissed his chin and moaned with every thrust. His mind was blank and black as the pleasure consumed his memory; her tight, young pussy throbbed and squeezed his cock with every thrust. Finally, Thomas opened his eyes and looked over his shoulder to see a couch in the center of the room; he pulled out and let Trixie down. Thomas turned and took off his shirt, kicked his boots off, and then took off his pants. Trixie moved to the couch as she lay on her back as Thomas joined on top of her. Trixie placed her hands on his shoulders as she moaned and quivered with every thrust. Thomas shook the whole couch with each thrust, sweating and pumping, moaning, and thrusting. He could feel her cum and tense with pleasure several times. Finally, Thomas got off Trixie, grabbed her ass with both hands, and motioned her to turn over.

Trixie willingly turned and buried her head into the cushion. She let out a gasp as he sent the whole shaft deep inside of her and began to thrust with his hand on her hips. She could feel a swell of pleasure; he reached around her waist with both arms. Both covered in sweat, they continued to fuck until Thomas felt the second load building; he pulled out of her and shifted his cock to her mouth where Thomas stroked his cock hard and shot his cum on her lips and face.

Just about that time, Thomas felt a tap on the back of his head, and the room began to spin. Thomas closed his eyes only to open them again to find himself face down on the table at the bar. He slowly raised his head and looked around to find a row of bottles lining the table with Trixie looking at him with an abandoned glare of disapproval. Trixie said, "Hey, where did you go? We were talking and drinking. I went to the ladies' room and returned to find you passed out with your head on the table."

Thomas looked around the bar and asked for the time as he swayed, trying to stand up. He said, "I will drive you home," holding the keys in his hand.

Trixie asked for the keys and said, "I invite you to my place until you sober up a bit."

Thomas, remembering his time passed out, smiled, and said, "Sure, lead the way."

Tim walked down an old tractor path leading up to the main road across from the drive-in, watching the corn sway in the wind as he looked forward to seeing Susie. Tim walked past the drive-in, and from behind the row of bushes and fencing, he found a spot underneath to sneak in. Stepping from behind the tall screen, he soon blended in with the crowd already there. Tim looked around

FERTILE DIRT STUDIO

and approached the concession area where most of the kids hung out, and that's when Tim heard a voice from behind him shout, "Stove Top!" As Tim turned, he saw Ricky and Susie with a group of other kids. Tim paused before walking toward them, remembering what his dad had said to Mr. Clark over the phone, but Ricky and Susie approached Tim as Tim began to speak.

"I am sorry about my dad."

Ricky said, "It's OK; I told my father that it was your sister and that your dad has been crazy since the war. Let's not worry about that, Stove Top; let's get some pizza and find a place to hang." Tim felt relieved as he followed them in line. Susie turned and winked at Tim and waited for him to catch up before holding out her hand. Tim grabbed her hand and felt relief over this night as he looked up at the stars and smiled. The three friends sat on the swings in front of the screen, eating pizza and watching the feature.

MOLLY STOVER

Susie watched Tim's every word and smiled as she scraped the ground with her feet. Tim looked at his watch and knew his time was running out. Soon he would have to leave to meet Molly and make it home before his father.

Molly walked through the alley and onto the porch to the back door and proceeded to knock. Moments later John opened the door, and Molly smiled and kissed him on the lips. They went through the house and up the stairs to his bedroom. The room was lit red, and a cover on the bed was covered with rose petals. Molly sat on the bed and began to remove her shirt. John asked Molly to stay the night, and they could explain to her parents tomorrow. Molly, feeling pressured, placed her shirt back on and told John, "I am not ready for this, and we can't do that—not yet!"

John got upset and hit the wall as Molly ran down the stairs and out the same way she came in. John ran out after her when he realized the sweater tied around her waist fell on the ground. He picked it up and sat on the porch facing the alley and hoped for her return. Molly ran down the tracks out of town, thinking of John being older and controlling her when she was unsure if she loved him.

Far enough out, she stopped running to catch her breath and turned to walk to the crossroads meeting place. She took the stone road between the cornfields, looking up at the drive-in lights off in the distance. Finally, reaching the crossing, she sat on an old rock in the ditch and began to cry.

Standing up and pacing on the old road, she decided to walk the rest of the way to the drive-in. Finally, she got to a hill overlooking a cornfield and chose to cut directly through the field to her destination. Molly entered slowly, carefully walking between the swaying rows down the hill into the area. Stopping for a moment, Molly heard movement in front of her. Unable to see clearly in the darkness, she kneeled and watched for feet in the flicker of light from the moon in between the rows. *Could it be an animal?* she thought. Maybe a deer or groundhog or even a skunk. Molly heard the movement around her as she turned herself to follow. Crouching lower, she began to feel frightened. Turning again to follow, she realized she lost her direction and was unsure where the drive-in was; Molly decided to run.

She started to dash down the row as fast as she could, feeling with her hands to guide her in the darkness. Not sure how far she had traveled, Molly slowed slightly but not before tripping on something in the row. Landing face first on the ground in the dirt, Molly laid flat for a minute; the only sounds were those of her catching her breath and her heart racing. For a moment, things seemed calm to the point that Molly thought maybe the images and noise were her imagination, and it was nothing at all. Finally, Molly decided to stand up and brush off, shaking her head. The darkness behind her emerged green, like fresh corn stalk, with a tall, slim, smooth skinned frame, black button eyes, and double-rowed jagged teeth. The creature grabbed Molly by the shoulders. Then it climbed on her and bit into her neck. Before Molly could even scream, she fainted from the shock. The creature released its bite, grabbed Molly by the feet, and dragged her away into the night.

Molly regained consciousness, woke up cold and naked, and left her eyes closed—pretending to still be out and trying to listen to her surroundings. She could hear crunching and chewing from her left side and barely opened one eye to see. Then, in the darkness, she saw an old woman on a pile of bodies, chewing and picking out pieces to cast aside. The woman seemed unaware that Molly was awake as it was wholly engrossed in the flesh. Molly, feeling terrified, decided to slide off whatever she was on and make a run for it. Molly opened her eyes and jumped onto the floor; looking back at the jagged rock slab, she turned to run toward the opening. As she approached it, she was stopped by two men—at least they looked like men—but their eyes were blackened and skin as pale as the moon. They grabbed her and pushed her into an unfathomable pit in the earth; she tried to get a foothold but couldn't.

Then the woman looking down at her began to vomit, soaking her with bits of blood and flesh. Finally, the woman stopped and jumped into the pit on top of her. Resuming the vomit, Molly continued to get covered, and as she did, the woman began to stick to her body like glue and proceeded to bite her neck, this time almost entirely in half as the woman gorged on her blood. She felt her life fading; her mind escaped this reality, and she began to see images of her mom in church and her dad asleep on the couch, her brother smoking on the roof, then black like she was free-falling into darkness, and then a drowsy nothingness. The creature's body and Molly's body began to merge, melting into a gelatin cocoon of blood, flesh, and bones. The two men covered the hole with a wooden lid like that of a coffin, leaving darkness below.

Tim looked at his watch, smiled at Susie, and said, "It has been nice seeing you!" As he got up off the swing, Susie stood up and kissed Tim on the cheek as Ricky smiled from behind her in between chomping on popcorn. Tim turned and ran for the fence, shouting at Ricky as he stopped and climbed underneath and off across the road. In no time, Tim's top sprint halted as he reached the crossroad. He looked around for Molly as he leaned against the boulder in the ditch. Tim stared at the moon and kept checking his watch. No Molly in sight. Tim began to get restless and annoyed. He turned to walk back toward town to check out John's house until he noticed a shoe lying in the gravel. He walked up to the shoe and realized it belonged to Molly. Tim picked up the shoe and saw it was covered in dirt with spots of blood on it. In a panic, Tim looked around in the darkness and began to sprint toward town and home. Thoughts raced through Tim's head as he got closer to town. Tim made it to his street before stopping to get sick on the curb and making it the rest of the way home. He ran his way into the house, calling out for Molly, Mom, and Dad; the house sat empty and dark.

Tim ran to the kitchen and the refrigerator to get the police number from a slip of paper in case of emergencies. Tim ripped the paper off the fridge and went to the living room phone. Calling the number, Tim contacted the dispatch, and before the officer could say anything more than hello, Tim said, "My sister is in trouble, and I need help!" The officer got the address and reassured Tim as she collected information. Tim told her about the night's events. Tim finished, hung up the phone, and waited on the porch, holding the bloody shoe. The police arrived, and Tim begged to go with them as he provided them the address of John's house.

Two officers stayed with Tim as he told them where the shoe was found. Tim sat on the porch as the other car waited with the officers in front of the house. The sheriff's department joined the search as Walton and Mills arrived, and they went through the cornfield and attempted to locate where the struggle took place.

Mills turned to Walton between walking the rows looking for evidence and said, "Are you sure this one isn't in the trunk?" as Mills winked.

Walton's slapped Mills on the back of his head and said, "Are you fuckin' stupid? Do not mention that again!" Walton grabbed the handle of his pistol and said, "Do you understand me?"

John was sitting in a chair, still holding the sweater, when he heard a knock at the door. John, thinking it was the return of Molly, opened the door with the shirt in hand and got hit by a man powerful enough to knock John out. Scooped up by the mysterious figure, John was carried off over his shoulder into the night. The police arrived at John's house and found the front door open. The officers drew their pistols as they slowly entered the house. They searched only to find no one in the house, just Molly's sweater lying on the floor. The police gathered up the shirt and placed it in the bag and continued to search the property.

Tim stared at the street, waiting for word about his sister as the patrol car sat in front of the house, and the officers waited for Tim's parents to return. Tim went into the house, looked in his sister's room, began to cry, and walked back to his room; he collapsed on his bed and cried to sleep.

TRUTH IS STRANGER THAN FICTION

Martin sat in his car as Sheriff Davis arrived. Davis walked to Martin's car and got into the passenger seat.

"Did your team find anything from the Fraley home?" Martin said.

"Just some blood and signs of a struggle," Davis said. "The press will get wind of this real soon."

Martin looked at Davis and said, "We already have a blackout on all local media regarding this investigation. I have contacts at the federal level that guarantee suppression."

Davis said, "How do you know this won't leak?"

Martin looked at Davis and said, "Because I have seen this before. Have you ever heard of Boston, Ohio?" Martin looked at the sheriff and said, "What I am about to tell you is all true and extremely confidential." Martin paused before continuing and said, "You will not share this with anyone if you expect you or your wife to make it to retirement." Martin spoke again and said, "My team has always thought we investigate cults, and I have never told them otherwise. I was assigned to a secret government agency team in Boston, Ohio. We encountered on the surface a cluster of devil worship activity. But it was all designed to cover the root of pure evil." Martin continued as the sheriff sat quietly listening. "There is a creature that is perhaps older than man. It is a form of mutated amphibian and can cocoon with its prey and emerge camouflaged. It looks like the person it takes and even retains the memory. But it needs human blood to keep the cell genesis active. These creatures live among us. These creatures avoid sunlight without makeup because the light breaks down the collagen, leaving them translucent and pale. They are not the stuff of Hollywood or religious dogma. They are living, breathing creatures. We encountered these creatures in Boston and evacuated the town after discovering a hive underneath. We quarantined all of the citizens, sorted out and stopped these creatures, bombed the colony, and sprayed the area with DDT."

The sheriff looked at Martin in disbelief and said, "So what do we call these creatures?"

Martin said, "They have been given several names over time; some say *vampire* or others say *wendigo* or *skinwalker*. We call them *Ube* due to their ancient origin."

The sheriff looked at Martin and said, "How are you so knowledgeable on these creatures?"

Martin said, "The federal government has been monitoring and studying them since they were first discovered. I was led in Boston and saw firsthand what they are. Some of the survivors that were Ubaid were quarantined and moved to Wright Patterson. I was present when they dissected, questioned, and tested these creatures."

Martin continued to educate the sheriff. "They are intelligent master manipulators and need queens to form a hive. These queens are rare and lay very few eggs. The DDT has been proven to kill the larvae by compromising the development. By blending in, they help ensure their survival and want nothing more than to have live births. Therefore, they desire humans to evolve and grow their numbers. So far, we have not tracked any live birth, but it only takes one evolved combination to change everything. They seek to mate with humans. That is why they find young girls to inhabit. They live deep underground and build vast tunnel systems and hives right under our feet. We aren't sure how long they live, but they feed on human flesh to produce the enzymes necessary to complete their transformation. The proteins are fat-based and allow them to make a sticky fluid that causes our cells and their cells to break down and combine into something hybrid. They have been thriving here with natives since before Europeans arrived. Once they decide to leave a body, they cocoon and find a new victim. This allows them to lead several lives. I am not sure how they retain memories, but only a small portion looked mutated when examining the brains. I am no doctor and can't begin to understand the biology of this. I just know they must be stopped."

Martin looked at the sheriff and said, "If we are to save this town, I will need you to understand all that I have told you and coordinate your deputies and cooperate seamlessly with me, or else the federal government will send in the rest of the unit, and this will become Boston all over again."

The sheriff sighed as he looked out the window at the corn blowing in the wind and said, "Not sure that I get it, but I understand."

Thomas woke up on the couch at Trixie's apartment and looked at his watch. Trixie was asleep in the chair. Thomas walked over, touched her wrist to let her know he was leaving, and thanked her for allowing him to sober up. Trixie smiled and said good night as Thomas stepped out of the apartment. Trixie said, "You are a good man, Tom Stover. Don't forget that." Thomas got in his truck and drove home. As he pulled into the drive, he saw the police car, and as he got out, the officer approached him to inform him that his daughter may not be missing yet, but they cannot find her.

Thomas said, "I told them not to leave the house!" He walked into the home and ran to Tim's room as he nudged him to wake up. Tim turned and looked at Thomas with his bloodshot, teared-up eyes, and Thomas started to cry, saying softly, "I told you not to leave the house."

Jane and the doctor were asleep in bed as the phone rang, and the doctor answered, it was Thomas on the line asking, "Who is this and where is my wife?" The doctor laid the phone down and shook Jane awake, whispering that her husband was on the phone, and he answered it!

Jane grabbed the phone off the bed and said hello as Thomas said, "Whatever is going on there, we will discuss later. Molly is missing, and the police haven't found her yet."

Jane, in a panic, said, "I will be right there," as she hung up the phone and began frantically packing her things. The doctor asked her what was going on; she told him, and he asked if there was anything she needed. Jane responded, "I may need a place to stay. I will tell Thomas the truth!"

The doctor responded," But my wife?"

Jane screamed at the doctor as she slammed the door and got into her car. She was lost in thought as the car raced down the road toward home.

FERTILE DIRT STUDIO

Martin Donnell arrived at the Stover house, rubbing his eyes from the night of searching, stepped out of his car, and surveyed the morning's calm. Martin thought to himself how deceptive the calm could be. Martin stepped on the porch and knocked on the screen door to have the front door open, revealing Thomas in his morning robe with a cup of coffee in hand. Martin produced his badge and introduced himself as Thomas opened the screen to let him in.

"Have you found her?" Thomas asked as the two men made their way into the kitchen and sat at the table.

Martin looked directly at Thomas and spoke calmly. "Mr. Stover, did you know she had a boyfriend?"

Thomas looked down at his coffee and back at the detective and said," I had no idea."

The detective placed his hands on the table and said, "We have recovered her sweater at his house, but the place was empty." The detective leaned back and said, "Maybe they left and eloped?"

Thomas raised his head and made a fist before relaxing his hand and said, "How did you find out about the boyfriend and where he lived?"

The detective said, "Your son gave the officers the location. Apparently, he had some knowledge of this existing relationship."

Thomas hollered Tim's name repeatedly before Tim appeared at the kitchen doorway. "Tim, you need to be honest with this man and answer all of his questions!" Thomas demanded as he got up to gather more coffee from the pot. The detective watched as the coffee was poured. He desired a cup but feared that Thomas would fight over coffee and realized he was more than the detective could handle.

Tim noticed the detective's interest in the coffee and said, "Dad, this man has been up all night looking for Molly; how about we get him some coffee too!"

Thomas turned and looked at the detective and said, "I am sorry. My son is right. We appreciate all that you are doing; this has just been a difficult night." Tim sat at the table as Thomas provided a cup of coffee to the detective along with a spoon and sugar container.

The detective looked at Tim and said, "Did your sister say anything to you last night?"

Tim looked at both men one at a time and said, "She told me she was tired of the rules and wanted to run away."

Thomas said to the detective, "Is that what you think this is? A runaway?"

The detective paused as he sipped his coffee and scooped in sugar. "No, I do not believe that at all."

Thomas, confused, said, "Please tell us what the hell is going on here." The detective began to construct a theory for the audience. "I believe Molly went to her boyfriend's but didn't stay, and she left looking for Tim. Maybe to say goodbye and run on her own—or maybe something worse. Tim found her shoe, and it has already been sent to the lab to be tested, but it contained blood on it. I believe the boyfriend, this John Walter, is somewhere looking for her, and he could be part of it."

Thomas looked at the detective and said, "Part of what?"

"This area has been a hot spot for satanic activity, and I am afraid your daughter has been led in and abducted." The detective looked at Tim and said, "How well do you know John?"

Tim replied, "I know that he loved Molly and made her happy."

The detective said, "Well, then maybe he went looking, and they both have been abducted."

Thomas said, "Abducted for what?" as he made a fist again.

The detective replied, "These cults use people for sex, get them hooked on drugs, and brainwash them. In some cases, they kill them when they don't conform."

"Why am I hearing about this now?" Thomas said, pounding his fist on the table. "Where has the sheriff's department been?"

The detective said, "They called me as this activity increased, and my team has been involved for a week. I believe Molly was in the wrong place at the wrong time and maybe her boyfriend too." The detective said, "I believe you had a run-in with Claude Fraley?"

Thomas paused and looked at Tim and then the detective before replying, "Yes, but that is over now."

The detective said, "More than you may realize. We believe that Claude Fraley and his boys have all been murdered by this cult. We found blood and signs of struggle in the house and on the property. We have also found signs of struggle, like the scene in the cornfield and at John Walter's place." The detective proceeded, "I don't mean to erase hope, but I wanted to give you all the facts."

Thomas looked at Tim and said, "Can we join the search?"

The detective smiled and said, "I would encourage that as you both might think of some place we haven't. This will take everyone's effort if we are to find Molly. I must be going. I have plenty of searches left and effort to coordinate. Thank you for the coffee. I will show myself out and leave you two to sort all of this out. If you need anything at all, please contact the sheriff's office to get me the message." Martin left the kitchen and made his way to the porch. Closing the doors to the home, he took one look back as he stepped off the porch and knew that based on the department's direction, it was time for federal intervention as he got in his car and drove off in the direction of the sheriff's department.

Thomas looked up from his coffee after the screen door slammed and said, "Detective?" toward the doorway's direction. Jane appeared at the entrance to the kitchen. Thomas looked at Tim and motioned his head in the direction of the doorway for

Tim to leave. Tim walked past Jane as she patted Tim's head. Without a look he walked up the stairs and disappeared into his room once more.

Thomas stood up and looked at Jane with an angry stare. "So, you and the doctor?" Jane nodded without a word. "How long has this been going on?"

Jane shrugged and said, "A few years."

Thomas said, "Did you know our daughter had an adult boyfriend?"

Jane said, "No, I didn't."

Thomas looked at her and said, "Well, maybe if you weren't such a whore and a better mom, our daughter wouldn't be missing." Thomas picked up a plate from the counter and threw it against the wall.

Jane startled and said, "Well, maybe if you weren't such a hard-ass, she would have talked to you."

Thomas grabbed another plate before placing it back on the counter and said, "I want you out of it!"

Jane said, "That's fine. I was leaving you anyway."

Thomas leaned against the counter, looking out the window, as Jane walked down the hall, stopping in the bedroom only to gather up her clothes from the closet. She placed them in an old suitcase that she had when she was sent to Indiana. Jane left the bedroom, looking up for Tim before passing the kitchen and out of the front door onto the porch. Jane looked up at Tim's window, trying to get a glimpse of him before loading her suitcase into the wagon. Jane got in the driver's seat and began to cry as she backed out and headed down the street. Tim came back down to the living room, fully dressed, to find Thomas ready as well. Thomas looked at Tim and said, "Take this backpack," as he pointed to a camouflage one sitting in the recliner. Thomas slung his rifle, and the two walked out the door. "Throw that in the bed," Thomas said as Tim placed the backpack in the front of the fender.

Jane arrived at the roadside motel as she entered the clerk's office to check-in. Paying with what cash she had from Toledo, her thoughts were focused on her daughter as she signed for the room. Not making any conversation with the clerk or nearly any eye contact, Jane left the office and walked down to her hotel room. Jane, tired from the morning events, placed her bag against the wall and closed the door, locking it behind her before lying on the bed and drifting off to sleep.

Thomas and Tim arrived on the dirt path behind the drive-in theatre outside the fence, almost where Tim had snuck in last night. "I want you to show me exactly where you walked to meet Molly," Thomas said as he got out of the truck, followed by Tim. "Grab the backpack," Thomas said as he looked over at Tim. Tim grabbed the pack and placed it on his shoulders as he began to walk with Thomas following.

They crossed the highway and onto the dirt road, pausing when they noticed the field and road full of searchers. The road was lined with police, sheriff, and state agents. They walked down the road as they looked at the cars and searchers they passed. Thomas grabbed Tim by the shoulder and said, "How far is the Clark Farm from here?"

Tim pointed to the railroad tracks and said, "It's about two miles down the tracks."

Thomas took the lead, clearing the cars and searchers to the hill and onto the tracks. Thomas surveyed the landscape and cornfields before he looked at Tim and said, "Let's walk away from this crowd further down and see what we can find." Tim followed as Thomas began to lead them further away from town. Thomas slowed his pace, allowing Tim to walk by his side as the two looked around for any sign of Molly.

Thomas looked at Tim and said, "Am I a bad father?"

Tim looked at his father and said, "No, Dad, but Molly and I have been afraid to make mistakes."

Thomas said, "There are rules, Son, and this is the reason why."

Tim lowered his head and said, "We are paying for our sins. This whole family is one sinful mess. This is our price, just like our last sermon in the church as a family." Tim stopped his dad and said, "We are not a family anymore; this is all of our faults." Tim began to cry before continuing to walk. Thomas looked at Tim as he walked ahead and followed, striding to catch up and placing his arm around his son.

John awakened to see men eating a human carcass on the floor; it felt like several days had passed in this underground room with a pit in front of him, tied to two poles with his arms outstretched. John could hear what sounded like breaking, followed by the strong smell of ammonia in the air. John could see fingers sliding out from underneath the wooden cover, sliding it off the pit.

Molly slithered out of a pit as she crawled slowly across the floor to John's feet. Her body glistened in the dim light, and her eyes flickered yellow. She unbuttoned John's pants as she crouched at his feet and slid them down, exposing his penis. She looked up at John with her yellow eyes and opened her mouth, revealing her sharp rows of teeth. She bit into John's cock as he screamed in pain; she drank and slurped his blood as Molly continued to bite all the way up his abdomen, chewing out flesh, guts, and blood. She went all the way to his ribs before stopping to reach in, rip out his heart still beating, and begin to eat it. Time was up. John was dead, and Molly was a beast.

—

Thomas and Tim reached the field behind the Clark Farm. Tim looked at his dad and said, "Maybe we should ask the Clarks for help?"

Thomas looked at Tim and said, "No time; we have already been out here for hours and have found nothing. Let's look this area over, and we will double back."

Tim went silent, trying not to argue with his father. They moved into the field in between the rows as the breeze caused the corn to sway. Thomas stopped as they reached a small runoff from the river at the end of the field. The water swirled into a large hole that swallowed up the water and created a current.

Thomas looked at Tim and said, "Stay right there," as he made his way through the shallow bed and to the hole. Thomas asked for Tim's bag. Tim removed it from his shoulder and tossed it to Thomas. Thomas kneeled and removed a flashlight from the bag before throwing it back to the edge of the field. Thomas shined the light into the hole and watched the light disappear into the depths. Thomas got closer to the hole and heard the voice of his dead brother calling to him. The voice called, "Tom, you left me to die." Thomas got closer with his head and shined the light closer to the hole as the water continued to flow past his feet.

Thomas had images of his brother flickering in his mind as he called out to Tim.

Tim looked at his father and said, "I am here, Dad." Thomas backed up from the hole, and before regaining his sense, Thomas realized it must have been in his mind and sighed as he looked back at Tim.

"We will need the Clarks after all," Thomas conceded. "I need to call the investigators, and we need to find out what Mr. Clark knows about this runoff and that hole." Thomas got up and walked to the bag, placing the flashlight into the bag before throwing it back to Tim. "Let's go, kid," Thomas said as he walked back the way they came.

Jane woke up from her nap and looked around the quiet hotel room. As her thoughts raced through her mind, she decided to search for her daughter. Jane left her room, got into her car, and began to drive down the road. Lost in thought as she drove, she finally passed a familiar place, and she decided to stop. Jane looked at the May Carry Shop from her car as she fixed her hair and makeup before leaving her car and walking into the shop.

Jane tensed up with anger when she saw the clerk who fucked her. The clerk, noticing Jane entering the shop, made eye contact with her, and turned and walked to the shop's back. The clerk stopped and turned, looking at Jane with remorse and fear firmly planted in his eyes. The clerk said to Jane, "Come with me." Jane hesitated at first before the need for answers took over. Jane followed the clerk through a doorway leading to a small table. The clerk looked at Jane and said, "You may want to sit for this."

Jane sat as the clerk looked directly at her and told her that the other guy that fucked her was his stepbrother. He also told her that the rituals were about the pagan expression of sex and anarchy—not harmful or evil. Then the clerk said, "The other night, we were in the woods with a group that we had only met recently. My brother Benjamin took his clothes off, and before the rest of us could join in, the cops showed up. We poured leaves on the fire, and I lost track of Benjamin in confusion. But, as I was running away, I ended up on some train tracks. I found a place in some bushes by the river underpass and decided to hide and wait things out."

Jane looked frustrated and said, "Why do I hear your problems? I have plenty of my own and need to find my daughter."

The clerk grabbed Jane by the hand and said, "This has to do with her."

Jane paused as her eyes began to tear and said, "Well, then tell me, dammit. You fucking pig, you owe me this!"

The clerk proceeded to tell Jane the rest of the story. The clerk said, "As I was sitting in the dark, I saw my brother being led by the others in the group to a small entrance under the bridge opposite from where I was. It's hard to see because it's overgrown with bushes, and it's right at the edge of the creek coming from the river. I think this group is real Satanists. I could hear my brother scream from the tunnel, and he hasn't been back since. I am scared they are coming for me. So maybe your daughter fell victim to these people. I didn't go to the cops because they will think I am a part of this, and really, in some way, I am."

Jane sat back and wiped her tears and said, "Where is this place?" Deciding to check for herself, she got in her car. Jane counted the cash left over in her purse as she thought of what was needed to search properly. *If I find the entrance*, she thought, *I could alert the sheriff and leave the clerk out of this.*

Mr. Clark's truck arrived behind the drive-in as Thomas and Tim got out to greet Sheriff Davis and Martin. Thomas turned and motioned Mr. Clark to wait as he turned back to greet the two men.

"I have found a large hole behind the Farm where the runoff is draining," Thomas said as he used his arms in a circle to measure. "Mr. Clark can show you where it is as he was surprised when we showed him earlier." Thomas looked at Tim and said, "We would go with you but have been out all day, and I need my son home. This has been hard on us, and we should be there if Molly makes her way back." The sheriff and Martin watched as Tim and Thomas got in their truck and drove off the dirt road.

"I think he doesn't want the kid to see us drag his dead sister out of a hole!" Martin said as he looked over at the sheriff. The two men got in the car as Sheriff Davis hollered at Mr. Clark from the driver's window. "It's getting late; we will follow you." Mr. Clark turned his truck around and drove down the dirt road, followed by the sheriff and Martin.

Mills sat in his car parked directly in front of Martha. The evening had faded and was consumed by night. The low static from the radio was the only noise in the car. Mills sat with his head resting against the door and his eyes closed. Sleep almost caught him before he was startled by a thumping sound. Mills looked around and waited for the thump to repeat. The thump did repeat, and it sounded like it was coming from the trunk. Mills panicked as he began to think maybe he was right. Maybe Walton stuck the missing girl in the trunk. Maybe that was why he took the night off. Maybe he was going to frame Mills for all his actions.

Mills got out of the car and walked to the trunk. "Are you in there?" he said as the trunk thumped again to give a response. Nervous and startled, Mills shook as he searched for the right key to open the trunk. Finally getting the key, Mills said, "Hold on. I will get you out." As the trunk lid opened, it did not reveal what Mills anticipated. It was the hitchhiker that was in the trunk days before. She climbed out as Mills backed away. Her skin was gray, and the hole in her head was nothing but a black spot.

Mills said, "We killed you. I am sorry."

The hitchhiker said, "I am back better than ever," as she looked at the deputy with her dead, droopy eyes. Mills reached for his pistol and got it tangled in the holster before it fell to the ground.

The hitchhiker said, "Going to kill me again?" as she jumped on Mills and said, "My turn!" before biting into his neck with her razor-sharp teeth. Mills collapsed as the hitchhiker drained the life right out of him. She dragged his body up to Martha, pushing him down into the darkness. The hitchhiker grabbed the keys from the ground and closed the trunk before getting into the car and driving away.

Martin and Davis stood over the hole as they turned to Mr. Clark, who stood at the edge of the field. Davis said, "We will take it from here. You can go back home." Clark nodded as he raised his lantern to guide him back through the field.

Martin looked at Davis and said, "We will see what's down there, and if this is a hive entrance, we will get out and arrange for us to take over this farm and get the reinforcements needed." Davis agreed as Martin got down on his knees, shining the light into the hole. Martin began to slide himself feet first into the hole before disappearing altogether. Martin shined the light around, seeing a large tunnel that was tall enough for him to stand up angled downward into the earth.

Martin hollered up to Davis to join him as he moved away from the entrance and waited for Davis to drop in. Davis dropped down and landed in the shallow pool of water collected from the draining water from above. Davis stood up, shined his light around, looked at Martin, and said, "How will we get back out of the hole?"

Martin said, "I am sure we are in the hive, and there is always more than one way out. So, keep quiet and follow me." Martin continued to walk down the muddy tunnel as the sheriff reluctantly followed. "This is proof," Martin said. "And even my team doesn't know about this. They think we are hunting cults. The truth would cause too much panic."

The two men came to an opening with three tunnels leading in different directions. Martin paused and said, "I say we go this way," as he pointed to the tunnel on the left. The men continued down the path into the dark. Martin grabbed his gun from his holster as he heard a noise ahead. Davis followed suit as the two-armed men moved slowly along the wall to a spot where the tunnel turned. Martin stopped and whispered to the sheriff, "I think we should turn back." As Davis backed up to turn around, a creature emerged from the muddy wall in front. Startled, he shot, striking the creature in the chest as it fell to the ground.

Davis turned his light toward Martin and said, "I got one," as two creatures grabbed Martin, who screamed and fought as he was pulled down the tunnel into the darkness. The sheriff turned the light back to the creature he shot to see it face-to-face. The creature bit Davis's face before he could shoot again, and three other creatures joined the feast and began to bite at the sheriff as he fell into the muddy earth.

FERTILE DIRT STUDIO

Jane arrived at the dirt road across the cornfield where the clerk said the opening was. Jane grabbed her flashlight as she got out of her car. Jane moved under the bridge, wading through the shallow creek. Jane found the narrow opening, sliding inside to a series of steps that led to the ground. Jane paused as she noticed drawings of snakes and people on the walls before seeing a dull light further down. Jane walked to the opening to a large room and saw John—the man's remains—and a stone slab with Molly stretched out and still. Jane slowly walked up to Molly as she opened her eyes and said, "Mama." Then her eyes turned black. Her mouth widened with fangs emerging from her gums. Grabbing Jane with a strong grip on the arm, Molly turned off the stone and bit right into Jane's neck and began draining blood from her as she tore at her neck while other creatures emerged from the darkness and began biting Jane's body until she was on the ground being ripped apart and eaten.

In his office, the doctor looked over in the corner of the room where a bag of items Jane left in the hotel sat. The doctor decided to get up and look through the belongings. He pulled out a pig mask under some other items; as the doctor turned over the pig mask, he noticed a tag that read the *May Carry Shop*. The doctor stared at the cover for a moment before deciding to go to the shop to find out if they knew where Jane went.

Thomas woke up on the couch, walked down the hall, and found Tim asleep. Thomas wrote a note to Tim telling him he would return soon. Thomas got in the truck and drove to the dirt road by the drive-in as the sun rose. He parked his vehicle off the road, grabbed his rifle, canteen, and flashlight, and sat on his tailgate, staring off into the field.

    He could see the rise in the area just before it slid downhill to the drive-in. Grabbing his supplies, Thomas began to walk toward the drive-in through the field and down the hill. With his rifle drawn, he slung it as he came upon a spot where the corn was broken and smashed with traces of the dirt swirled up. As he examined the earth, he saw what looked to be clumps of dried blood. Thomas followed the path of blood through the field away from the drive-in, further away from town, leading him to the train tracks before the trail disappeared. Thomas looked both directions down the tracks and decided to walk further away from the town. Before coming to a creek bridge, he noticed what seemed to be tire tracks in the ditch by a side road. Thomas walked to the ground where the soft dirt was and examined the marks. Stopping to look around at the creek and the bridge behind him, Thomas decided to walk back down the tracks toward his truck.

HELL TOWN

Donnell stood at the entrance of a sizeable concrete storm drain big enough to walk upright into darkness. He was flanked by two soldiers; the radio blasted from one of the soldier's belts. "We are ready for you to bring him in."

"Roger that," the soldier replied as he hit the talk button cabled onto his Kevlar. The three men stepped into the tunnel as the soldiers turned on flashlights to guide the way. The men slowly tracked through the knee-high water as Donnell carefully trudged in the dim light provided. His thoughts ran wild. *Am I being executed?* he thought. The surface had been evacuated. All reasons had not been revealed; maybe he had already seen too much. Martin looked at the two-armed soldiers and thought, *Perhaps I should make a run for it?*

The soldiers noticed his suspicious demeanor as Captain Olivia spoke up and said, "Don't worry. If we wanted to shoot you, we would have done it outside the tunnel," as Sergeant Gonzalez laughed.

The men grabbed Martin by each shoulder and nudged him a bit as the captain said, "Let's keep moving. We are almost there." The tunnels turned into another shaft with a solid door and red light above. Gonzalez knocked on three times as a small slide opened. A voice on the other side said, "The Rooster doesn't lay eggs," to which Gonzalez replied, "The rain won't last forever."

The door made a loud series of bangs as it opened, and the overhead light turned green. Olivia and Gonzalez turned and walked back the way they came as Donnell was greeted by two more armed soldiers and a woman in a white lab coat.

The woman spoke first, "Hello," she said. "I am Dr. Amy Castle. I am in charge here, Martin, and the reason you are joining us." Martin began to introduce himself and was quickly interrupted. "I know all about you." Amy spoke as she stepped sideways in the room and said, "Now, if you will follow, my time is limited, and I have much to show you." The group walked into another room where there was a cell set up behind a glass wall. This room was clean and brightly lit, and the cell sat empty except for one young boy. He was strapped to a chair. Martin studied the boy as he sat in the chair.

"He's not crying," he said as he looked at Amy. "What kid sits chained to a chair in a cell and doesn't cry. How old is he?"

Amy looked at Martin and said, "The boy was about eleven, but what you see here is much older." Martin got a puzzled look on his face as Amy began to explain herself. "Have you ever heard of *klepto-genesis* or *recombination*?"

Martin shook his head in confusion.

"It is the stealing of DNA from one species to another to modify the thief entirely. What if I were to tell you a creature living among us since the beginning uses this to camouflage itself and live like us?" Amy added as she looked directly at the boy.

Martin shook his head and said, "I would have to say bullshit."

Amy looked at Martin as she called out to the soldier, "Soldier enter the cell and show Mr. Donnell what we already know!"

"Yes, ma'am!" the soldier replied as he walked to the steel door and opened the cell.

Martin watched with curiosity as the soldier closed the door, turned, and shot the boy several times in the chest. The boy's head dropped as Martin looked on; he was confused and disgusted. Then the boy raised his head, exposing black eyes and razor-sharp teeth. The soldier left the cell to rejoin the doctor and Donnell.

The doctor said, "There you have it."

Martin said, "What is it exactly?"

The doctor said, "Pure science," as she explained more. "People have called it many things, most popularly *Vampire*. But what it is and what it does are unique. This creature has amphibian and human cells that are evolved. Its brain is highly developed, just like our own. It is a scavenger that stores protein in its body by ingesting flesh and fat. This conversion helps it change from what it was to a humanoid."

Martin looked at the doctor and said, "How the hell does that happen?"

The doctor said, "These creatures historically would grave rob recently dead and cocoon—like a caterpillar—using enzymes and the protein to create a living hybrid with the dead host. Since the modern method of embalming has improved, they prefer live hosts."

Amy continued to explain as she looked at the creature. "Somehow, with a live host during the cocooning, they can tap into the memories, making them almost perfect.

"Almost?" Donnell asked as he looked at the creature. Amy turned on a bright floodlight from a switch overhead. The light shined on the boy with intensity.

"Now, look closely," Amy said. "See the translucence in the skin?"

As Donnell looked closely, he could almost see bone through the white flesh.

Amy said, "That is their one flaw; the protein chains do not make durable skin cells. They continue to need blood to help with this condition and eat a person down to nothing to provide what they need."

Martin said, "How do you know all of this?"

"My father first discovered them in Turkey. He was an amateur archeologist. He believed these creatures sprang from early Ubaid and Mesopotamia were looked at as gods; he went to Turkey, where he encountered many writings and artifacts. This led him to discover a secret path deep into the earth. This is where he found several cocoons of these creatures and a den. My father returned and told the government what he saw; they locked him up and said he was crazy. It wasn't until they encountered these hybrid imposters elsewhere that they began to believe."

"Where is your father now?" asked Donnell?

"He was here as we are standing in the middle of what was a den. I have lost contact with him and fear he may be dead. These need our disguises to survive. The queens are few and only lay a few larvae before becoming infertile. They are trying to propagate as hybrids to achieve live births, and the day that happens, we are all in trouble. They are highly evolved, predator, intelligent, and adaptive. They are deadly in their natural form, but they are more lethal with a more developed brain as a hybrid." Amy walked into another room as Donnell followed.

Amy removed the sheet, revealing the creature. Martin studied the creature with curiosity as a slight rush of fear filled his senses. He divided his attention over waiting for Amy to provide details and the appearance of the beast. Amy grabbed a chart from the metal exam table as she began to speak.

"This creature is about five feet in length, and as you notice the shades of green like a frog," Amy produced a pointer from her pocket as she pointed at the hands and feet. "My first thought was a reptile until I saw this. Five fingers and five toes," Amy said as she continued. "When we ran it through a series of X-rays, we revealed that its skeleton is very much like our own. The blood and tissue samples we tested all indicated amphibians with human similarities."

Amy put down the pointer and grabbed a scalpel as Martin kept his attention fixed. Amy cut a thin membrane on the creature's abdomen, revealing a cavity where she reached in and pulled out two mucus-covered eggs.

"These creatures are asexual and only reproduce in small amounts like these two quarter-size embryos. But not all of them reproduce, leaving the rest to be drones and workers." Amy placed the eggs in a dish and set her clipboard beside it along with the scalpel. She wiped the mucus from her hand onto a white towel and continued by picking the scalpel back up. Amy then cut into the chest cavity as clear fluid poured from the wound and onto the floor. Like a professor, she recited her book knowledge from memory.

"Osteoclasts are multinucleated monocyte-macrophage derivatives that degrade bone. Osteoclasts dissolve bone minerals by massive acid secretion and secrete specialized proteinases that degrade the organic matrix in this acidic fluid."

Martin looked at Amy and said, "What the hell does all this mean?"

"These creatures become us by dissolving our cells and bones into liquid, then combining into a hybrid like that thing sitting in the other room. They do so by cocoons, like caterpillars, and the true metamorphosis takes place. I find that proteins found in this process are of the flesh of humans. They need flesh and water to make this happen. These bags of fluid sit right underneath the lungs, and they vomit on their prey to start to begin the change. So, they feed and fill these bags and then seek out the victim. Not all of them seek to be a hybrid as once they make the change, they can no longer produce eggs. But they have been trying to copy us for a long time to produce a live birth. If they accomplish this biological leap, we are all in trouble. They are strong as a hybrid as you saw in the other room; they regenerate body parts like a salamander as the cells they contain are almost all fibroblasts, and I believe that is the key. Somehow, they potentially fed on a human in the past, which created a mutation. That mutation over time evolved into what we have, and it is a natural way of survival. We have a record of dead people returning as a hybrid, which is regeneration on a whole new level," Amy expressed with conviction.

Martin stepped back from the table as he looked at Amy, then again at the dead creature, and said, "OK, let me get this straight. These are mutant killer frogs that want to take over?"

Amy shrugged and said, "Yes, in simple terms, and it sounds crazy when you say it. Why do you think they locked my father up before they found proof? These things have been here for thousands of years, maybe even prehistoric. But they live deep in underground caves and live undetected. They can continue over many lives because they are made of fibroblasts, even as a hybrid. I don't think they completely copy memories, but somehow through a cellular memory, each new victim they take has access to the short-term memory while still having a part of the human brain rewired and intact. They can store those memories over many victims in their core brain stem. They need to feed on us to stay as humanoid. The cells age and break down; they find another host and take over. Hybrids are not asexual as the process changes them to be more like us. But the males cannot produce semen, and the female's eggs have not yet evolved to be compatible with human fertilization."

Amy looked at Martin as she laid the scalpel down on the table. "We evolved over millions of years. This is the next evolutionary contender, and if we aren't careful, this will be our successor. My father wasn't the first to discover these creatures. In Los Angeles, tunnels and caves were discovered deep under the city almost fifty years ago. They were confused with lizard people and, of course, discredited as nonsense. These things have been fictionalized in books and myths. Vampires, they say, because they had no other explanation for what they were seeing. We are a secret agency of scientists and soldiers crested to deal with this rising threat. Some of the myth is true. They don't like garlic because it affects their ability to hunt by scent. They have a collagen deficiency as a hybrid which, as you saw, if they don't feed, the skin cells break down, and they become pale and translucent. So bright light can reveal them in between feeding; that is why they prefer to hunt at night and are rarely seen during the day without makeup or massive feeding. Finally, there is holy water. They thrive in fresh water. But salt water is toxic and dehydrates the affected area rapidly, causing the skin to crack and bleed. Therefore, the town has evacuated all residents and given the bright light and blood test, and those that we found were executed and burned, except for our guest and a select few, the boy we found scouting around here a few hours ago."

"Why do you need my help?" Donnell asked as he looked at Amy.

"We believe this is the beginning of further infiltration into Ohio. We need you to keep an eye out for strange activities. You can build a team, but you must keep your real mission a secret and only involve others on a need-to-know basis because these creatures are hiding among us. If you require any support, contact us directly through this number."

Amy passed Donnell a card that he read briefly before placing it in his pocket. Amy said, "We will be finishing here soon and returning to Wright Patterson to monitor from command. Good luck and be careful; in two weeks, come to visit for further examinations, and we will help you establish a cover and build a team." Amy motioned the soldiers to escort Martin out of the complex. Martin followed the soldiers out of the maze of tunnels. Outside in the open, as he stared back at the entrance before moving on, Martin pulled the card from his pocket and sighed as he walked away. Martin felt sickness and anxiety come over him as he walked further into the daylight.

Olivia stopped Martin and said, "We have something to show you." The three men walked down a ravine and arrived at a large cage covered in a camouflage tarp. The soldiers pulled off the tarp, revealing what looked like a buck's head with a humanoid body. The creature was large, half deer, half humanoid with brown fur and fingers and toes in place of hooves.

Olivia shrugged and said, "After we evacuated, we caught one that tried to combine with a deer, and this was the result!"

The creature snarled and growled as it shook the cage and spoke. "Let me out of here, and I will make sure you get spared. The queen is here, and we will reign!" Gonzalez locked his rifle as Olivia placed the tarp back on the cage.

"We are taking this to the base for studies," Olivia said as he finished up. Olivia shook his head as the beast continued to talk and growl. "You should see what happens when they combine with a wolf!"

NO TIME TO SEARCH FOR DEAD WHORES

Thomas made it back to his truck and placed his rifle on the seat beside him, and drinking water, Thomas decided to wait a bit before leaving. Feeling tired, Thomas put the gun on the floor. As the cool breeze flowed from the truck window, Thomas drifted off into the black. Thoughts faded like water rushing down a drain. There he felt Jane's touch on his cheek, struggling to react. Thomas peeked with his eye as he sat up. Before he could ready himself, he smelled death like rotten meat. Jane was sitting next to him; gnarled and nasty, she placed her hand on his face as she struggled to speak. "Thomas, they will kill you too," she said. "It's not her," Jane began to repeat herself. "It's not her…it's not her…it's not her…"

Thomas opened the truck door and fell out, hitting the ground before waking up drenched in sweat from the dream. Thomas focused on the cloud-covered setting sun and the chill of the fall Ohio air. Thomas placed his coat back on, grabbed his rifle, slung it over his shoulder, and stepped out of the truck to stretch while looking at the road ahead. Thomas paused as he saw lights approaching from the distance and thought maybe this could be the sheriff. He turned, placed the rifle in the truck through the window, stood by the engine hood, and waited.

As the lights approached, it was that of a car. Thomas stepped away from the hood and walked in front of his truck to get a better look. Finally, the car stopped, and it was Dr. Brady. Thomas recognized him as Brady got out of the vehicle.

Thomas grabbed his rifle and said, "I figured you would be somewhere comforting my wife."

Brady replied in a nervous tone, "I am looking for Jane. She left her bags at the hotel; one of the bags had a mask from May Carry, and when I went to visit them, they told me that she was headed to a bridge out here."

Thomas remembered the bridge a mile back by the tracks and urged the doctor to follow him. Thomas got back into his truck and drove down the road with the doctor behind him. Thomas wondered if he had missed something and wondered why the doctor was so concerned; he was fucking Jane and didn't love her. They both arrived at the end of the road by the field before the bridge. Stopping his truck, Thomas got out, followed directly by the doctor. As the daylight faded, both men stood looking at the area for anything odd. Thomas walked over to a set of tire tracks that he had noticed before and showed them to the doctor.

Thomas looked directly at the doctor as he turned and stood up. "So, you fuck my wife, wreck my family, and right now, all that matters is Molly. You want to help me, then help me to look for her!" Brady lowered his head away from the angry eyes of Thomas's gaze.

The doctor said calmly, "Yes, I was with her for a while. It was her idea. At first, I refused, but she was very persuasive, and from then on, I became addicted."

Thomas shook his head as he walked toward his truck to grab his flashlight and rifle for a more prepared search; the doctor followed him, thinking of the words to say next. When out from the fading light, a man jumped on the doctor and began to tear at his arm. Thomas turned with the rifle and light saw the carnage and the doctor screaming for help; Thomas aimed and fired directly at the man on top of the doctor, landing a shot right in the man's back.

Thomas cocked his rifle again and aimed, but the man jumped, landing several feet away, and ran off into the field. Thomas turned as if to pursue the man but stopped to attend to the doctor. "That man looked like Martin," Thomas said to the doctor, who was bleeding from his arm.

Thomas had already torn his shirt and took a piece of it to wrap the wound tight to slow the bleeding. The doctor told Thomas that the man was biting at his flesh, and he had no eyes. Thomas helped the doctor up and prepared to walk him to the truck. But, before he could say another word, a voice came from behind him. Thomas picked up his rifle and turned in the direction of the voice. Before him stood Ayaz and Allen Mercer. They told Thomas that he was in danger, and so was his son.

Ayaz said, "Take the doctor and get your boy and meet me at Allen's cabin."

Allen revealed the location. "It's on Old one-ten beyond Parkers covered bridge. When you see the dirt road that goes up the hill to the woods, you will find a pond and beyond that, the cabin." Ayaz and Allen resumed pursuit down into the field, vanishing from sight. Thomas asked the doctor if he could drive, and the doctor nodded. Thomas told the doctor to follow him home to get his son.

Tim sat home waiting on the couch watching television, focusing on the noise to stop feeling totally alone. Tim was stirred by this, then a knock at the back door. Thinking it was Thomas drunk, Tim walked down the hallway and into the back porch leading to the door.

Tim felt his pulse race, and his stomach turned as he pulled back the curtain, revealing Molly. Molly looked at Tim and asked him to unlock the door and let her in.

Tim smiled, then frowned, and said, "Where have you been?"

Molly smiled and told Tim that she would explain everything as she shivered and said, "It's cold; please let me in."

Tim started to turn the lock, and in a glimpse, he saw something different from Molly—something he could not explain. Her eyes flickered black for a moment as she watched his every move.

Molly said, "Tim, let me in, and I will fuck you before I kill you brother fucker!" she laughed. Exposing the razor-like teeth in her mouth.

Tim ran from the door as Molly began tearing through it. Tim ran into the kitchen and climbed down into the pantry, hiding behind the shelf where it gapped just enough for him to slide into. Things went silent as the tearing stopped as Tim tried to make sense of what he just saw and calm down.

Thomas opened the front door and walked through the living room; looking around, he noticed the back door shredded and smashed in pieces. In a panic, Thomas called out for Tim. Tim hesitated to answer as he was not sure about anything or anyone. Thomas shouted at Tim again, "We have to go now!" Tim slid out of the pantry and crept around the corner toward the entrance to see Thomas standing in the living room. Tim called out to his father and said he saw Molly, but it wasn't Molly those eyes and teeth! "Dad, it wasn't her."

Thomas grabbed Tim and ushered him out the door and guided him to the truck. Thomas then shouted to the doctor, "Leave your car. Come with us. We are going to need a truck." The doctor climbed out of his car, holding his blood-soaked arm and medical bag, and got into the truck with Tim and Thomas.

They drove off into the night with many questions of each other and minimal answers.

The doctor spoke of his arm doing better and how the man that did this seemed unusually strong, and his teeth were like razor blades. Tim spoke of Molly and how it seemed like her until her face changed, and the eyes were black like holes. They passed through the old, covered bridge down the old road. They drove up the hill and into the field before reaching the pond and the old cabin—buried and overlooking the valley. They unloaded the truck and made their way inside the cabin. Thomas grabbed some dry wood from an old supply box, placed it in the fireplace, and started a fire. Tim asked his father what this place was, and Thomas replied, "Some friends invited us here. Hopefully with all of this, we can get some answers." Thomas pointed out the food on the table and the wood stocked in the box as he went to a board with a map and markers on it.

Thomas made his way to a closet, and as he opened it, he stopped in surprise. Inside was old hunting camouflage with a series of rifles. Thomas sat with the doctor and Tim on an old couch by the fireplace and said, "Now we wait."

Tim said, "What does all of this mean?"

Thomas said, "I am not really sure."

The doctor was already asleep, resting from his wounds. The night went on as Thomas fed the fire, trying to make sense of what was going on.

Tim finally shut his eyes to rest, and Thomas made sure the door was secured by placing a wooden board across the door into the holder before he moved to the rocking chair, covered up with his jacket, and fell asleep. The morning came quickly as the light made the dull gray of the cabin into its original color. Thomas woke up and looked outside before wondering about the man and his instructions. Before he could wonder much more, there was a knock at the door. Thomas grabbed his rifle and walked to the door as Tim and the doctor woke up.

Thomas motioned for Tim and the doctor to remove the board as he aimed his rifle directly at the doorway. The board was removed, and Thomas shouted, "Come on in." The door creaked open slowly, and there were Ayaz and Allen from last night. Thomas said, "Come in. Sit down. I want some answers," as he followed the men with the barrel of his rifle. Ayaz and Allen took a seat on the couch as Tim and the doctor closed and secured the door.

Ayaz said, "You come to feed the fire and sit; we have much to talk about." Thomas lowered his gun and motioned Tim and the doctor to sit. The man said, "Let me introduce myself. My name is Ayaz Arslan. I am not from this land, but I have been here for many years. You are all confused about what has been happening; let me tell you what I know.

"I was once a child in Turkey, and the village that I lived in spoke of many things—very dark and evil things. Legends of years ago, something emerged from the ground around Denizli. This creature was much older than man and lived hidden in darkness. But, somehow, this changed; the creature had mastered a way to look like us and resemble our traits while killing us and eating our flesh like livestock. I grew older in the village. I realized that this creature existed because of my brother. There were stories and legends about how such evil erased the surrounding villages.

"My village fell victim to these creatures. When they came and killed everyone. I lost my family and left in search of the truth and survival. I call them *strayer* as a reminder because that is how they left me—homeless and wandering. I traveled to Europe and even into old Transylvania searching for answers but found nonsense. I know they are among us in great numbers. They will continue to infiltrate your neighbors and friends until they are either strayer or dead. Legends would call them something supernatural. They are not any of that. My brother was a victim. The creature that took my brother, Asil, is still out there somewhere. I came to America and have tracked the beast here. We need to kill all the queens before any more die. They will kill everyone you encountered; they hunt by scent and are very effective at what they do. This place is many miles from where we have tracked, and they will finish up killing close by before they spread."

Tim interrupted with one name "Ricky! Dad!" Tim shrieked in fear. "The farm! Ricky is right in the area. I have spent time there. My scent is all over that farm, and I have been walking that area and those tracks for months; maybe I am to blame?"

Tim broke down and began to cry as the men looked on.

The doctor opened his medical bag and started rewrapping his arm after an injection of penicillin and said to the group, "Maybe we should teach these animals a lesson."

Ayaz nodded in agreement and said, "I have been here for many years hunting and destroying these monsters. I am sorry about your wife. I believe she is gone, and I am genuinely sorry about your daughter; she is with the queen now, and they will stop at nothing to destroy us all and continue quietly moving about, taking what they want."

Thomas looked at Tim and the rest of the group and said, "Let's finish this!"

They grabbed all the weapons they could carry. The group headed outside where an old van sat as the daytime began to fade. Ayaz said, "We will hunt in this," as he pulled open the sliding door to reveal even more weapons. "They are nocturnal hunters, like most predators, and sleep during the day; we need to hunt them tonight while they are scattered, and we need to find the den and save who we can."

The group gathered in the van; past the pond and down the hill they traveled.

—

The Clark family was settled in at the dinner table, eating and talking about weekend plans, when a knock came at the door. Mr. Clark got up from the table and opened it to find Molly standing in the cold, shivering. "Molly!" Mr. Clark said, "Where have you been?" as he let her into the house.

Ricky and his mother came around the corner when they heard Molly's name. They stood looking at Molly in disbelief as she said, "I was lost and somehow found my way here, have you seen my dad?"

Mr. Clark replied, "No," as Molly frowned and said, "Could you please call my dad?"

Ricky said, "It has been days; where did you get lost?"

Molly said, "I fell down a hole and lost my soul," as she smiled and began to repeat herself louder and louder. Molly smiled and stared at Ricky.

Mr. Clark was dialing the phone but stopped to ask Molly if she was all right. Molly smiled, and her mouth began to sprout rows of razor teeth as her eyes turned black, and the front door slammed open with two men who attacked Mr. and Mrs. Clark as Molly jumped and landed on top of Ricky, forcing him to the floor. The two men began to tear at the flesh of the parents, splattering blood, and flesh all over the room.

Molly looked Ricky in the eyes and said, "We are going to eat you last," as she swiped up blood spatter from the floor and licked her hand clean of it. Ricky watched in terror as his family was being massacred with no way of stopping it.

FERTILE DIRT STUDIO

Molly was too strong, and he felt her hand digging into his chest. Molly moved in on Ricky's neck, and before he turned his head, she bit out a piece of flesh, leaving him bleeding out on the floor. Ricky held his hand over the gushing wound and began to cry; the hunters came through the door and began to shoot at the creatures with everything they had. Molly picked up Ricky and threw him at the men, and the strayer ran out the back of the house into the field.

The men started to chase but stopped as Tim was screaming, huddled over Ricky. The doctor and Ayaz placed pressure on Ricky's wound as Tim knelt beside him. Ricky looked at Tim as his breath faded and said, "Stove Top," before dying. Tim began to cry and scream as he held on to Ricky's hand. The strayer came back from behind the house and sprayed the house's back with gasoline from the farm pump and then threw a lighter at the home, instantly igniting the property in flames. The group of hunters fled the house as the fire consumed it quickly. Pulling Tim back into the van against his will, they drove off into the night.

STRAYER

The two boys ran down the hill away from the flock, racing to the next hilltop. As they stood over the grassland, they could see the village down the path. The sheep flooded the valley behind them. The boys ran over the next rise as they played, and the thick clouds' shadows moved over the land. Asil ran to a pile of rocks, climbing up as he laughed. Ayaz tried to catch him but collapsed with laughter from the silliness of his brother. Asil stood at the top of the rock pile, raising his hands to the sky. The boys' afternoon was interrupted by calls from their father, who was off in the distance from where they came; Asil began to step off the rock hill but tripped and fell as he caught his foot in a hole. Ayaz ran to tend to his brother as he tumbled onto the ground. "Asil," he said, "are you OK?" as he stood over him with concern.

Asil stood up quickly and jumped on his brother as he laughed. The two boys ran, laughing and shoving each other along the way. The hole in the rocks collapsed even further. From the depth, it came slowly, the small green body climbing out into the light. Its black eyes were watching the boys as they faded into the distance. The creature turned and looked back at the hole as it growled and ran in the brothers' direction.

The boys arrived at home as they walked single file into the house. They nodded to their father as they walked to a bucket of fresh water to wash before dinner. Finishing the wash, they adapted themselves at the table and sat well, waiting for dinner to arrive. Their father spoke as he stroked his long black beard. "I want you boys to stay away from the hills on the southern path. There are ruins in those hills from those who lived here long before us." The boys looked at Father as he spoke.

"When I was a boy, my friend Mert wandered south into the hills, and the elders said he became lost. I could hear them talking. Those evil spirits had stolen his soul. We must protect ourselves from wicked boys and follow the rules."

Both boys nodded as their mom brought dinner to the table. Father grabbed the first helping of *kofta* and *yufka* as he passed it around the table. The family ate as the evening faded. The boys cleaned the table, covered the leftovers in the pantry, and washed up the dishes well before going to bed. The boys put the dishes on the rack and walked to their room.

The room sat between the main house and barn, two small beds lined with straw and one blanket on each. Ayaz set the lamp in the center of the floor as he waited for Asil to settle in his bed before blowing out the light.

"Tomorrow, brother, it is my turn to herd the flock," Ayaz said as he got comfortable.

Asil giggled and said, "My big brother, all alone with all the sheep."

Ayaz chuckled and said, "Soon, little brother, you will be twelve, and it will be you."

The boys rested for the day ahead. A noise in the barn awakened Ayaz. He tried to look for his brother in the dark but could not see him. He grabbed the lantern and went to the kitchen to search, sneaking past his parents' room as they slept. Borrowing a flame from the hot coals in the *tandir*, Ayaz used a stick to light the oil lantern and walked out the front door quietly into the night. He slowly walked around the outside of the hut, passing underneath two windows as he quietly moved along.

Climbing over the small fence and into the barn, Ayaz looked for the source of the noise among the wagons and bails of straw. Stepping as far as the light would reach, Ayaz walked behind a cart near the far corner of the barn. That's where he saw Asil kneeling in the corner, feeding grain to something in the darkness. He extended his hand and returned it to a small bag to grab more before reaching back out.

Ayaz whispered to his brother, "What are you doing feeding the rats?"

Asil turned and looked at the lantern and Ayaz and said, "No, I have made a friend." Asil looked back at the darkness and said, "My brother wants to meet you too," as he grabbed the lantern from his confused brother and directed its light on the corner. The small creature tensed as the light gave it away. Its green skin and black eyes reflected the illumination of the lamp.

Asil scooped more grain into his hand and extended it as Ayaz watched in disbelief.

"It seemed hungry when I found it," Asil said as the creature carefully ate from his grasp, trying not to wound him with its small sharp teeth.

"I must get Papa," Ayaz said. "He would know what it is."

Asil said, "I already know what it is, my pet," as he smiled. "If Papa knows, he will kill it or drive it away," Asil said as he rubbed the creature's head. "I will keep him hidden in the barn and feed him late at night. I will name him the moon," said Asil as he raised his hands.

Ayaz became intrigued as he studied the creature. "I will not tell, but do not feed it alone, and it must stay hidden in the barn." Asil smiled as he told the moon to hide. The creature crawled to a pile of straw bales and slid in between them out of sight.

FERTILE DIRT STUDIO

Ayaz said, "Well, now let's go back to bed!" as the boys walk back into their room and bed once more, extinguishing the light of the lantern.

The boys grabbed and slipped into *peshtemal* from the walkway before entering the bathhouse room where the heated pool steamed from the hot coals shoveled underneath. The boys dipped in the water as they slid down to soak, dunking their heads underwater and laughing softly at each other's expressions through the steam. Finishing the bath on time, the boys switched from the soaked cloth and into their clothes and off to breakfast. A breakfast of eggs, cheese, and warm milk awaited. Father sat, already finished, as their mother cleaned the dishes away from the end of the table. She seated herself near a closet in the hall to eat.

"Boys," Father said as he watched them eat, "Today, you will lead the sheep to the river and watch over them. Ayaz, tonight, you will lead them to the pasture and camp." Asil smiled as Father turned to look at him and smiled back. "Soon, Asil, you too will herd the sheep," Father said. "I am going to be in the north fields today with the wheat."

The boys finished eating as Father continued to talk. They got up from the table; one by one they took their dishes to Mama before walking to the barn. The boys grabbed the crooks hanging on the wall as they walked past the pile of straw. Asil shoved his crook underneath the bale, lifting it slightly to discover the edge of a hole and several rocks surrounded by loose dirt. Dropping the bale back down, he looked at Ayaz with a puzzled expression. The two boys left the barn and went into the sheep corral as a slow series of clicking noises came from the bales. The boys opened the fence gate as they drove the sheep out, running down the stone path. The boys led the sheep and dogs down into the valley across the meadow and to the river. They sat on a rock as the sheep huddled by the water's edge, drinking and grazing.

The meadow's cool breeze kept the sun from becoming too oppressive as the boys ventured off the rock and chased each other around, fighting with one another using crooks as swords. They stopped as they sat by the water's edge, laughing as they ate some bread and drank water from a flask Ayaz carried from home. The day drifted as Ayaz whistled for Khan and Battal, their Kangal sheepdogs, lying at the edge of the herd.

The dogs got up and began to bark as the boys led the way back up the hill and across the meadow. The village's return seemed more extended than the morning departure as the boys ultimately made it back. They drove the sheep back into the corral and the Kangal back into the pen that sat to the hut's back. They washed up from the well by pumping water into a bucket and dipping their hands in, washing clean hands and faces and hooking up the crooks as they passed by the bales of straw and through the hall into the hut. Mama greets them as they sit at the table.

"Papa?" Asil questioned as he looked to the front door.

Mama said, "Maybe later. The field must have him busy." The boys ate lamb and *tarhana* as they sat quietly with Mama. The sun set as Ayaz rounded up Khan and Battal once more before opening the gate to the pen. The two dogs rounded the herd and followed Ayaz to the meadow for the night. The backpack of sticks and a mat sat high on his back as he kept his lantern hooked to his crook with flint stuck inside his belt. Ayaz couldn't help but wonder about Father as he crossed the path leading north before heading down to the grassy meadow. He looked one more time in that direction; with no sign of anyone, he began to set up camp at the last site he used.

Ayaz removed sticks from his pack and arranged them in a stone pit laced with handfuls of the tall, dry grass from the top of the hill. Dogs kept the circle tight as the sheep huddled to graze and stay together. Ayaz grabbed the flint from his belt and lit the dry grass and sticks. He was feeding a small fire as he sat next to it for warmth. He was laying out his rolled blanket underneath him as he stared up at the stars. Ayaz added more to the fire as he became comfortable enough to drift off to sleep. His thoughts fell away as the slow fire burn illuminated the hilltop.

The stars faded slowly as the night gave way to the morning. The sun found its way to the small hill and onto the back of a sleeping Ayaz. Ayaz woke as he turned to look at the sun, flanked by a clear sky. He stood as he stretched, looking down the hill at the sheep still corralled by the Kangal. Khan ran up the hill to greet his master as Ayaz patted his head and said, "Let's go home and eat." Ayaz whistled to signal the two dogs to round the herd. He then rolled his mat up from the ground and placed the roll onto his back. Looking down, Ayaz finished off the coals from the fire with a morning piss.

He was looking in the home's direction as he finished and grabbed his crook and walked down to the path that began in the valley. The thought of home put a smile on his face as his stomach growled for food. Reaching the top of the valley, Ayaz stopped and stared with confusion. The clear line of sight had given way to a view of his village in the distance. Smoke filled the sky as homes looked to be on fire. The sheep and his grumbling belly became the last thing on his mind as Ayaz threw off his mat and cast his crook aside. He began to run with all his strength. The adrenaline had his heart beating hard like a drum in his chest. He halted himself just before the last meadow leading right up to his home.

The huts and stables were unrecognizable. The fire had destroyed and blackened everything. Ayaz, confused and upset by what he saw, slowly walked the path as sadness in his mind turned to danger. He crouched in the tall grass, peeking to see if anything or anyone was moving. Time had passed, and no sign of anything or anyone had left him curious and confused. Slowly he left the tall grass and made his way into the open. Lining himself along an old stone wall, he turned the corner and saw the remains of his home. The hut and barn burned, and smoldered smoke still filled the air.

The quiet absence of anything living heightened the horror of the surroundings. Ayaz approached where his home had been. He paused to notice the area where the straw was; it had turned into a large opening with the dirt and rocks around it burned black from the fire. Ayaz knelt at the edge of the hole as he grabbed a stick and threw it in. Hearing no noise of the stick landing or hitting a wall, Ayaz became bewildered as he looked around for any sign of his family.

He called out for Mama, Papa, and Asil with no reply. He heard a noise from the hole as a hand grabbed him by his clothing, and it began to pull. It was his brother, Asil. Ayaz started to feel relieved but felt horror as he got a better look. The face was pale, and as the light reflected, it looked green underneath the skin.

The eyes blackened, and teeth sharpened and protruded. Ayaz screamed as his brother began to pull him. Ayaz fought with all his strength, but his brother was powerful. He could feel his brother's grip tightening on his chest as they were almost face-to-face. Asil opened his mouth full, revealing rows of small sharp teeth. Ayaz closed his eyes as he began to cry and scream; a growl startled him as he opened his eyes to see Kahn leap and bite Asil on the neck, removing the grip his brother had on Ayaz. Asil and Kahn fell into the hole and faded to black. Ayaz crawled back from the hole as he could hear two different types of growls from the darkness. Ayaz got up and ran from the village the same way he came. He rejoined Battal, who ran beside him as they made it to the meadow's top. Ayaz grabbed his crook and mat, taking one last look at his home before nudging Battal as the two took the path north.

THE LAST ACT

"They're all dead," Tim screamed as he sat with the group. "Molly, the Clarks, they are all dead!" Ayaz placed his hand on Tim's shoulder as Tim began to cry and told him that he was about the same age when his village was lost.

Ayaz told the hunters, "We must stop this evil. Who else would the strayer be hunting?"

The doctor said, "I must go to my family."

Ayaz replied firmly and said, "No, now the queen has your scent. Any return to your family will result in them dying. She will be focused on us now! We must regroup and gather supplies." The group traveled miles from the fiery nightmare and back to the cabin.

Thomas got out and began to head toward the cabin to follow Tim but felt a hand on his shoulder. Allen stopped Thomas and said, "You help Ayaz and the doctor. I want to talk to your son." Thomas clinched his teeth but agreed as he turned toward the doctor, helping him out of the van. Allen walked into the cabin and found Tim sitting on the bed.

"Can I sit?" Allen asked as he looked at the chair in the corner. Tim shrugged as Allen took a seat. "I was ten when I lost my mother. She was killed while I was in the other room, and it was all my fault. I came here to live with my uncle, who was taken by the strayer because he wouldn't give me to them on my birthday. My uncle is one of them now, and they used his body for scout."

Tim looked at Allen and said, "How am I ever going to survive this? My sister, Ricky, and I don't know where my mom is?"

Allen stood up and said, "Stay close to your father; you are all he has too." Allen left the room as Tim laid down on the bed with his eyes open, somewhere between shock and disbelief.

The hunters gathered in the living room with weapons loaded by their side. Ayaz said, "Let's rest. In the morning, we will continue the search."

The morning came as Martin Donnell arrived at the courthouse with his team for a public meeting. Martin entered the courthouse and said to the clerk, "How does my makeup look?" as he smiled, trying not to reveal his true self by biting her and letting his predator's brain take over. Martin stepped up to the podium as Deputy Walton, District Attorney Rodgers, and Trixie flanked to the right and his investigators to his left. The crowd consisted of local reporters, business owners, and police. Martin looked down at the podium before looking up at the crowd.

"It is with great sadness that I stand here today. Last night Sheriff Davis was killed in the line of duty. There has been a long-standing cluster of evil in this county. Sheriff Davis contacted me over a week ago. We have identified the people responsible. This week has not been without its tragedy. We have had a total of seven missing persons, all presumed to be dead. This does not include the death of Sheriff Davis and the family of Ronald, June, and young Ricky Clark, whose farm was burned to the ground to cover the cold-blooded murders."

Martin walked over to a board on an easel, flipping a cover to reveal a list of names in large bold print. "This list is a credit to my team," Martin continued to speak. "The cult members responsible are led by a Turkish man named Ayaz Arslan, and the members are as listed Allen Mercer; Dr. Walter Brady; Thomas Stover; and his son, Timothy Stover. These individuals are responsible and are now fugitives from the law. I have been in contact with the federal government, and now the manhunt begins. I will be setting up a command center at the sheriff's department. We will be offering a reward of $5,000 for information leading to these cult members' whereabouts.

"To further assist this county in immediate support, I am placing David Walton in charge as the new acting sheriff. Together we will restore safety to the county and communities therein. I know many of you may have questions, but this is the most I can tell you for now as this is an active investigation. Thank you for your time."

The crowd murmured among themselves as Martin and his team left the small courthouse. Walton looked over at Trixie and said, "I knew that Thomas Stover and that drunk had something going. They must have killed Deputy Mills and took his car. This town will never be safer now that I am sheriff," Walton smiled while looking Trixie up and down. Trixie left the courthouse and stood out on the street, watching Martin and the investigators get into their vehicles.

Martin smiled at her as he placed sunglasses over his eyes before getting into the passenger seat of a truck as they left the quiet street. Trixie felt uneasy as she sat in her car; disbelief filled her thoughts.

Thomas woke up in the cold cabin as the fire died, and the other men remained asleep. He walked down the hall to find Tim absent from where he was. Thomas hurried down the hall and out the front door into the autumn morning. As Thomas looked at the wooded ridge, he spotted Tim on his knees over by the wood line in a small clearing. Thomas called out to Tim as he ran toward him. Tim stood up and turned toward Thomas, revealing a cross made from old boards with names scratched into it. Tim took the knife that he was using and dropped it to the ground as he wrapped his arms around his father and began to cry intensely.

"This is my goodbye to them," Tim said in between the tears. Thomas looked at the names on the cross and read them to himself. Mom, Molly, and Clark. Thomas looked down at his son and then at the makeshift cross; before he too began to cry, he looked at the morning sun.

"Come on, kid, let's go inside and warm up." Thomas turned and placed his arm around Tim as they both walked toward the old cabin. They looked up only to notice Allen, Ayaz, and the doctor standing at the cabin entrance. As they approached the men at the door, the men moved aside, allowing Thomas and Tim to enter before walking in behind them and closing the door.

The clerk worked steadily moving inventory in the stock room of his shop. When he heard the bell from the counter ring, the clerk walked from behind the curtain to find Molly standing at the counter.

Molly looked at the clerk with her face smooth with makeup and her lips bright red and said, "Is there somewhere quiet we can talk?" She undid the top button from her shirt, revealing the top of her breasts. The clerk was unaware of who he was sharing the conversation with. Holding the curtain back with one hand, he used the other to signal the invitation into the stock room. The clerk followed her as Molly turned to sit at the small table. Molly looked at the clerk as he sat at the table opposite of her. She reached for the small lamp cord hanging down and pulled it, casting light on the two and the table. "So much time spent in the darkness," she said as she smiled at the clerk.

"I am Molly," she said as the clerk looked on with confusion. "I want to thank you for helping me," Molly said as her eyes flickered black then back to clear blue. "It was the scent of this body and the nurse that was discovered when we had our ritual in the woods. I wanted this body; I could smell its youth and beauty!" The clerk's confusion turned to fear as he scooted back slightly in his chair, plotting a way to escape. Molly, sensing his tension, looked at the clerk and showed her teeth and black eyes. "No reason to run!" she growled. "You will see I am only trying to thank you." The clerk sat suspended in fear. Molly continued, "Let me tell you. As I am sure you already know that nurse tasted so good. I was going to take her body, but she was all used up by you, your brother, and many more." Molly began to laugh as she said, "I enjoyed feasting on her body." The clerk felt hands on his shoulders as he turned to look up. It was his brother, Benjamin, looking down at him. Molly smiled and said, "I am returning your brother better than he ever was, and you can be better too—if you want. But if not, I expect you to help, or else you will become another meal."

He looked at Molly as Benjamin squeezed the top of his shoulders. "Help with what?"

Molly smiled and said, "We need more food and don't want to get it ourselves. We need you to do what you did with the poor nurse. We want you to build a cult of followers and lead the tasty ones right to us. That way we can remain hidden, and you can have all the pleasure you desire."

The clerk looked at Molly and said, "Do I have a choice?"

Molly said, "Leave and we will find you; we control this land."

The clerk shuffled in his chair and said, "If you are so powerful, why do you need me?"

Molly's face changed back to blue eyes and innocent, and she said, "We have certain vulnerabilities that limit our power. We just want to live among you and survive. Will you please help?"

The clerk smiled and said, "This sounds like fun."

Benjamin released his grip, and the clerk placed his palms open on the table as Molly placed her hands in his. "I have been around for many years. Ilona was my last rise as queen," Molly said as she rubbed the clerk's hands.

———

Allen Mercer walked out of the field and up to the back door of the family farmhouse. Allen paused before he turned the knob and walked in. Sitting in her rocker by the fireplace, he saw his aunt resting. She opened her gray eyes and smiled. "Allen," she said, "did you find him?"

"No, Aunt, not yet," Allen said as he stood in the corner.

"You may not get your chance," Mrs. Mercer said as she reached out from her blanket and, with her old trembling hands, gave Allen a newspaper.

Allen stepped from the corner and grabbed the paper, reading the headline aloud, "Cult members revealed." Stunned, Allen threw the paper in the fire, kissed his aunt, and said, "We will have to leave now."

Mrs. Mercer said, "This may be goodbye, son." Allen walked out the back door and ran for the field as Mrs. Mercer watched from the window and rocked the chair.

The hunters, renewed, were loading up the van as Allen Mercer ran from the wood line. "They have blamed us," he said. "All of us are now fugitives."

Thomas looked at Ayaz and said, "They must be in control of the county now."

Ayaz said, "There is no time to waste. I have several safe houses available. We must leave now."

The doctor looked at Ayaz and said, "Where will we go?"

Ayaz looked at the team and said, "I have plenty of support in New Orleans."

Tim said, "What about our home and life here?"

Ayaz said, "Today, you all no longer exist. In New Orleans, we can get you all a new identity, but we must hurry. If the strayer has this county, that means we are vulnerable."

The hunters gathered supplies and left the cabin as they drove off in the van. As they traveled down the highway, Tim looked out the window, watching the county pass by. They passed the hitchhiker walking as they left; she smiled with her black eyes and sharp teeth exposed.

THE LAST TRUE QUEEN

Vlad looked from the tower as Ilona stood at the bottom of the hill among the bodies of soldiers and peasants raised on rows of pikes. She could sense his eyes on her as she licked at the blood. She walked her way back up the hill, bathing in the moonlight with her white dress blowing in the breeze. She walked in a circular motion up the torchlit steps until finally making it to the master bedroom and opening the large wooden door and stealing the attention of Vlad, who was seated in his chair, enjoying wine, and brooding over her presence.

"Tell me again?" he said as she sat on the edge of the bed.

"I will tell you, but you must stop asking and trust me!"

Vlad adjusted his position to sit more upright as he said, "I will rip you open to see what you are and place you out there with the rest of the bodies."

"When you stopped at that last village in my homeland on the way back here, I saw her arrive while I was on the hillside. You brought her to me. That night while you drank and slept and fucked the peasant girls, I took her away to a place where we could be together. The village has many tunnels underneath, and we returned as one in the morning."

"So, you are a demon?" Vlad asked as he narrowed his eyes.

"No, we are two that became one. I am still Ilona, just a better version of her."

"What do you want with me?" Vlad looked over at his sword.

"I just want you to give me a baby."

Vlad said, "We already have a son."

Ilona nodded her head and answered, "Yes, but he is from who I was before. If you do this for me, I will provide you with children that will rule the world. I already have an army hidden and waiting as I am queen of them, and you will be the king."

Ilona walked to the large, heated bath as she removed her dress and slipped into the water. Her white skin became transparent in the glow of the candles, revealing her pale, boney core.

"I must feed more on others to hide this. Vlad, please call the servants. I am still hungry and need fresh meat if we are to have children."

Vlad rang a bell as the queen blew out the candles. Two servant girls walked in as Vlad waved them to the pool. They saw the queen in the dim light as she told them to join her. They removed their robes and climbed into the pool. As they began to kiss the queen and wash her, she laid back with her eyes closed. Suddenly, she raised her head as her eyes turned black, and her mouth produced several sharp teeth. She held both with her arms as she bit rapidly, causing them to slump before eating their flesh right off their bones and drinking the blood.

Vlad watched without fear as his thoughts were regarding her as an equal. Ilona stood up from the pool, stained red from blood, and she grabbed the bodies, one in each arm, and took them to the balcony and threw them off. They dropped into the river below. She walked over to the towels. She wiped herself off and presented her naked body in the light to Vlad. Her skin was opaque and almond-colored like it was before the village.

She said, "See, I am powerful, and I can give you what you want; now give me what I desire." Ilona crawled up on the bed and stayed on all fours. Vlad got up, walked behind her, and removed his erect penis from his pants. Grabbing her smooth body with his rough hands, he penetrated her as deeply as he could. With every pump, it felt coiled and tight, squeezing him as he worked.

The queen moaned and growled as her nails dug into the bedding. Vlad backed up and turned her over to look at her face as he penetrated her. Her eyes turned black as she looked Vlad in the eyes. Even more tightening up on his cock, Vlad released a nut with a roar of pleasure. The queen smiled as her eyes returned to normal, and she laid back on the bed. Vlad pulled out as the queen sat up and said, "I want to drain you!" She placed Vlad's cock in her mouth and extended her jaw to take it in past his balls. Vlad, overcome with pleasure, became erect again. He pulled his cock and balls from her mouth and proceeded to fuck again. She didn't feel sloppy like he had been there before; all his nut had been absorbed. She was smooth and tightly coiled like before. Vlad looked at her as she smiled and kissed his forehead. One more tight squeeze, and Vlad burst again. This time staggering back after finishing, he sat in his chair with his drooping cock throbbing as it shrank.

Ilona got up from the bed, walked over to Vlad, extended her Jaw, and swallowed his cock and balls again. She was softly sucking as he ran his hands through her hair. His mind was flooded with ecstasy as he had never encountered, and his reasoning was to do whatever this queen commanded. "You are sent from God," he mumbled as she sucked.

"I am of the dragon, and you are the dragon. We are destined to be together." She stopped sucking and crawled upon Vlad, who stood erect.

"Go ahead, my queen. Drain me, and you shall have your child." The queen rode Vlad, bouncing hard off his cock, as he sat with his head back and her arms stretching on both sides. She thrust forward as her animal slit coiled, and she pushed back one more plunge down on Vlad, squeezing him of his last bit of juice. He let out his last gasp followed by a scream.

The queen rose off him, full of cum and content, as she made her way back to the bed and stretched her skinny almond body flat on her back. Vlad raised his head and looked at her, and said, "My dragon, how do I become like you?"

The queen turned her head as she spoke. "If you become like me, it will no longer be you. We do for our survival, not for the survival of who we become."

"But I already have no soul," Vlad said as he smiled at the queen.

The queen paused as she sat up on the bed and said, "I promise you I will never let you fall. You will be timeless, just like me. I have been many over this life. I stay until I begin to wither and then find another.

"This is how I discovered your queen. I was a withering villager who saw her youth and beauty. I had to have her and took what I wanted. This led me to you, and I believe you will give me what I want. I want survival for my kind."

Vlad listened as the queen continued.

"My nature has been here before man became what they are. We are declining on our own and need to adapt to survive. We have evolved and blended in with man, and slowly, we have grown in numbers."

Vlad, intrigued by her statements, said, "How? I want to know how."

"We came from the marshland exposed when the Ubaid tribes drained the land for food. They kept us like pets in our natural form, and we fed on the flesh of enemies they defeated. Slowly we emerged and became something different. They thought us a sign from the gods, and we were worshipped and idolized. I have been here since the beginning and am among the oldest of my kind."

The queen got up, grabbed the sword off the rack, and proceeded to cut off her other arm below the elbow. The blood did not ooze from her; it bubbled into a sac, slowly growing larger until it hung down the length of her missing arm. The sack began to swell until it burst to reveal a new limb as if nothing were cut. The queen picked up the old arm and threw it at Vlad as she stuck the sword back in the rack.

Vlad took the arm off his lap as the queen laughed and said, "Now imagine what we can do when we find someone we want. We feed on them, savaging the flesh, and inside the sac, we are reborn together. Neither the same—just become the one. I still can feel Ilona the way she was before. I have her memories and desires, but I am in control of this body." The queen noticed that the conversation had ended as Vlad was asleep in the chair. The exhaustion of being drained finally caught him. The queen crawled back on the bed, outstretched on her back once more, and shut her eyes.

Far from home and away from the queen for several months, Vlad looked down at his dead horse and grabbed his sword from the rocks. He turned as his enemy approached. The Ottoman scouts outnumbered him five to one as they dismounted from their horses and surrounded the king. His men were dead, and he had to fight alone as he raised his sword and lunged at the aggressors, dropping his shoulder in the motion. The first strike landed on his back as the Ottoman steel pushed into his ribs. He fell to his knees and looked to the sky, and said, "My queen, you promised I would never fall." The next sword took his head.

DEAD MEN SEE ALL THINGS

The diner was quiet; only a few patrons remained in the late evening and were calm. The man sat fixed on his cup of coffee. He thought to himself as he leaned back and began debating with the voices in his head. *I put sugar in the coffee; it's still coffee. Its murky black absence of color hid what was inside.* He looked over at the counter and watched the server interact with the cook in the back. *They appeared normal,* he thought, *but only on the surface. Were they hiding something underneath? Something dark and deadly?*

He shook off that thought as he looked out the window at his partial reflection in the glass. *It's good being dead—no one to answer to and no limitations on where to go, what to do, or how to do it.* The man turned from his reflection when he thought of his daughter. *This anonymity will help me keep her alive,* he thought. That was his mission—keeping her and everyone safe. His mouth twitched a bit as an involuntary reaction to his mental conversation. The man caught himself and looked around the diner to see if anyone noticed before getting up from his booth and laying cash on the table.

The server approached as he avoided eye contact. "Can you help? I am looking for a place to stay here in town and am just not familiar with this locale." The server pointed and gestured as she laid out directions, and the man quieted his voice long enough to follow and retain the instruction. Walking out of the diner into the fall Ohio air, his appearance with his dirty clothes and worn-down overcoat would be enough incognito for even the sharpest eyes. *His vagabond routine would end tomorrow*, he thought; as for tonight, getting in from the cold and a good night's rest would help him think more clearly.

The man brushed his salt and pepper hair from his eyes as he surveyed everything he had done for weeks as he arrived with a purpose in mind. *Ruddy*, he thought as he walked into the night. That is what his dad had called him. It was better than his given name, he reasoned. "Rutledge Danforth Castle," he mumbled as he shook his head—if his father could see him now. Ruddy approached the highway and made his way to the small motel lot, pulling a small stack of wrinkled bills from his inside pocket as he walked into the office. The ring of the bell brought the clerk.

Ruddy looked at the skinny clerk with his white shirt and clean-cut and timid demeanor, and said, "I need a room," as he placed the wrinkled bills on the counter.

The clerk softly asked with a lump in his throat, "Uh, do you have a name for the registry?"

Ruddy glared at the clerk and replied, "Yes, Joseph Stalin!" as he signed for the room.

The clerk frowned as he took the pile of cash he needed and turned the registry over to Ruddy for a signature. "It will be room thirty-six at the end."

Ruddy looked at the clerk and said, "I need scissors and a razor!" The clerk went into his private room and returned with a pack of disposable razors and scissors, laying them on the counter. Ruddy smiled and said, "Mother Russia, thanks to you!" as he scooped up the items and said, "I will be only one night, and do not disturb me!"

Ruddy made it to his room and sat on the bed, resting against the wall as he looked around the tiny room. Still stuck in his head, he began to recount what he had seen. He imagined a copy of himself sitting at the small table by the window. "Do you remember that night on the hill?" he spoke. "Those two deputies, what they did to that poor girl. The one is dead now; she returned as one of them and ate him down to nothing." Ruddy laughed and said, "That poor deputy cried like a baby!" *No, that's not how; it happened barely even a whimper the way I saw it. He didn't have enough time while it tore him apart.*

Ruddy shook his head and said, "Why did they go into the hole? That sheriff and the investigator—what a bunch of amateurs. I told them not to go but, they couldn't hear me from the field. I had to hide; they were all around." *It would be best if you had tried harder to warn them. Those screams that came out of that hole reminded me of when we were in that fox hole surrounded by Germans.* "These are not Germans," Ruddy said as he shook his head.

"That investigator is one of them now. I warned them all back in fifty-six after we came back from Turkey. They locked us up and said we were crazy," Ruddy said. As he grabbed his balls, "they shocked my balls to see if I was lying. Then all that LSD and locking us away for months." *But they learned. Sooner or later, they always learn. It was that president, that war hero, that survived the sinking of his ship. The only one left in the raft. That opened their eyes to the truth. Those eyewitnesses were not crazy. They saw him eating the other sailors and throwing their bodies into the ocean. He was a beast.*

"That's not how it happened!" Ruddy smacked his head on the headboard of the bed. "I was there when it happened passing by in the other raft!" *No, we weren't we were in France! That wasn't even real. I think it was a movie we watched. But we saved lives, American lives, and we were at war. We didn't save that family as their house burned tonight. That nurse and her daughter; what about her daughter? We know what she is. We just watched and waited. We could have told them all the truth and warned them. We could have saved this town. But here we are sitting, reminiscing. What about the group trying to stop all of this? They will be next. It wasn't like Venezuela; that was great.* Ruddy said, "Yeah, I even signed that bomb, the Rutledge bomb, and stood on the hill as it blew up the hive." *We are slipping, fighting in our fifties. We are too old for this.* "My daughter," Ruddy said, "I need to look out for Amy; she is smart but vulnerable. If they get a hold of her, it will kill me." That thought quieted the conversation as Ruddy laid on the bed and rested from his insanity.

Martin Donnell sat in the sheriff's department as he watched his team work to fine-tune the office headquarters. His hunger was swelling as he watched Trixie take her shift at the dispatch desk. Martin looked back at his team as thoughts of how long it would take to feed and change them all one by one. Maybe he could shift Trixie and make her a drone. He wondered what it would be like if he was a drone stuck with her body. Martin decided as he shook his head that he would eat her instead. His attention shifted to Walton as he watched him sitting in his office. Would he keep him as he is or allow him to become a drone?

There seemed to be something puzzling about Walton. Martin could feel a sense of a predator when he was around him; *after all*, he thought, *it takes one to know one.* His newfound human body allowed him to remember how complicated humans were. He nodded as he thought Walton was complicated and interesting. Martin stood up from his desk to address his team of investigators.

"I will need the six of you to come with me. We will do one last sweep of the crime scenes, including the Clark Farm, to check for any evidence we have failed to collect."

Walton stepped out from his office before Martin told David, "You and Trixie stay here to keep headquarters intact. We will radio if we need any duty support or you to assist directly." Trixie looked down at her desk, avoiding eye contact, as Walton returned to his desk. The team walked out of the office with Martin leading them.

Trixie looked at Walton and said, "How much more evidence can they find?"

Walton looked up from his paperwork and said, "Maybe a clue will lead them to the suspects." Walton proceeded to talk and said, "Trixie, I know you thought Tom Stover was a good dude, and perhaps his son was a good kid, but I assume they killed half of their family, and the weird part is we have been through that house and have found nothing other than a smashed back door. Now I wonder where they made all this killing. Then the business with Claude Fraley and his boys. Still no bodies but all gone, right after they had a run-in with the Stovers. They must have another location somewhere in the county that we have not yet located, somewhere with bodies stacked to the ceiling. Martin named them all as suspects, and he has been our lead in this. If he was wrong, why are they not attempting to clear their name? Do you know where they might be?"

Trixie shrugged and said, "No, Sir, I wasn't personal with the family. Thomas saved me from getting attacked outside of Damp's a few nights back, and he seemed like a nice guy. A little rough around the edges—but nice. Sheriff Davis thought he was a decent guy too, and just wanted to protect his family. Did you see what they did to Davis? His face was cut right the fuck off! They are going to keep that casket closed for sure!"

Walton smiled as he looked at Trixie and said, "Sheriff Davis lost his life because he trusted the wrong mother fucker, and when we close in on those savages, we are going to gun them down for sure!"

Trixie looked back down at her desk, turning her attention to the speaker's noise on the radio. She could feel Walton's eyes still fixed on her as she thought to herself, Was he right? Thomas and Tim—killers? What about Deputy Mills and his missing squad car? What would a cult want to be caught in a squad car? None of this made sense. Why did Martin seem different? What was his angle in all of this? Walton, as sheriff, did he really know who he placed in charge?

Trixie watched the clock as her mind wondered about Thomas. She looked at a map of the county on her desk as she studied the possibilities of his location. Her mind was convinced that he was not capable of what he was charged with. She hoped he was somewhere safe, and the truth got sorted out. She looked over at Sheriff Walton as he leaned back in his chair, looking out the window. She shook her head as she couldn't connect why a state investigator would place Walton in charge and not have his team take over. Puzzled, Trixie resumed her study of the map.

The door to the office opened as Trixie turned her attention for a greeting. "Hello," Trixie said as a woman approached her desk.

"Good afternoon. I am here to see Inspector Donnell."

Trixie looked at the woman as she looked around the room. "He isn't available right now. I can take a message, or you can talk to our acting sheriff."

The woman turned her attention to the sheriff, who was watching her with a blank look on his face. The woman looked at Trixie and said "Sheriff, it is!" as she nodded to him.

The sheriff interrupted the exchange and spoke directly from his office. "May I ask who you are?"

The woman smiled and said, "Forgive me. I am Dr. Amy Castle from Wright Patterson. Martin called me three days ago and said he needed my help. I have been unable to return his call and just figured I would make the drive today."

The sheriff stood up and walked out of his office and said "Castle, you don't mind my asking? What kind of doctor?"

Amy shrugged and said," I am a behavioral psychologist that specializes in human behavior." Trixie looked at the doctor.

The sheriff paused for a bit of silence before inviting her to his office. The sheriff walked back as Amy followed, and they both sat.

"Trixie, would you close the door, please?" The sheriff commanded. Trixie got up from her desk and closed the office door before returning to her seat.

"I could have got that," Amy said as she looked across at the sheriff.

The sheriff smiled and said, "That's OK; we have been quiet today with the investigators and deputies out searching. I have to pay Trixie to do something."

Amy turned and looked back at Trixie then again at the sheriff. "You must have a low opinion of women?"

Walton scooted in his chair a bit and said, "Why would you think that?"

"You appear to be in the late thirties, and yet I see no wedding band. Trixie seems polite and intelligent, yet while I have already gathered from my talk with Martin, this county is in trouble. She sits behind a desk when she should be out helping collect information."

Walton smiled and said, "Never met the right woman, and if you want Trixie to assist, you are welcome to have her show you the county."

Amy stood up and said, "That is a great idea. I will do that until Martin and the team returns."

The sheriff stood up as Amy walked to the dispatch desk and asked Trixie for help. Trixie looked at the sheriff for approval as he nodded before she followed the doctor out the office door. Walton watched through his open blinds as the two women left and mumbled "Cunts!" before returning to his seat.

Trixie walked around the truck as Amy got in the driver's seat. Seating herself in the passenger side and closing the door, she looked at the doctor and said, "Government plates? What is going on here?"

Amy said, "You show me the county and be honest with me, and maybe then we can talk. So, where should we go first?"

Trixie said, "How about where this all began at the Walton Farm?"

"Walton?" the doctor said. "Like the sheriff?"

"Yes," Trixie said, "his cousin, in fact."

As the two women left the parking lot, Amy said, "OK, lead the way."

―――

Captain Olivia sat at the table, enjoying a game of solitaire, as Gonzalez laid on top of one of the kings in the room. "This hotel sucks, sir!" Gonzalez said as he looked at the captain, waiting for a response.

The captain, continuing his one-man card game, barely flinched as he responded. "Yes, I agree. However, I would much rather be in the field taking care of business than held up here waiting for orders. I hope the doctor sees what she needs to confirm our mission—and quick."

"I hope this does not turn out like Boston!" Gonzalez said while looking directly at the captain with a concerned look on his face.

The captain stopped his game and said, "It's all about lessons learned, soldier. Eventually, we will outthink and outmaneuver these creatures.

"When I was in Vietnam, the cover was to prevent the spread of communism when really, the jungle was covered with these things. We burned the jungle down and waged a secret war. What we learned is these things are fragile in their somewhat natural evolutionary form before they turn hybrid. We change the environmental conditions, and they suffer. It's just a matter of time until they are erased. We can't allow them happening to make a successful leap into a fully functional humanoid. That is where the doctor comes in. The doctor and her father are the only hope of stopping this—more so Amy since her father has been missing for months."

Trixie and Amy arrived at Martha as the sun set. They got out of the truck as Trixie began her layout explanation.

"This started over there, along with a location just west of here on the other side of the field." Trixie pointed to the woods. "We almost apprehended some cult members during a ritual. This is all according to the reports I typed from the former sheriff."

The doctor surveyed the pit and the landscape. "Has anyone talked with the owner of this property?"

"I believe our current sheriff may have, and nothing unusual was ever mentioned."

"So, Walton is sent by the former sheriff to interview his cousin; meanwhile, folks continue to come up missing?"

"What about this Deputy Mills?"

"No one has seen him for days. And his cruiser cannot be located."

Amy said, "We have much to unravel here. I will take you back to the sheriff's office. Here is my card with hotel details on the back; if you think of anything unusual, contact me directly." The women got back into the truck and left Martha behind.

―

Amy sat in her truck across from the sheriff's office as the morning swelled into the day, finally watching Martin and the team as they arrived one by one, parking and entering the office. The wait was over as Amy crossed the street and entered the sheriff's department.

"Good morning!" she said loud enough for all to hear, and she opened the door. Martin and the team continued to work uninterrupted as he acknowledged her greeting by approaching her.

"Did Sheriff Walton tell you I arrived yesterday?" Amy asked.

Martin looked at Walton's empty office and said, "No, we were working the crime scene late last night, and I didn't have a chance to speak with Walton."

Amy studied Martin for a minute and said, "Let's use his office to talk."

The whole time she noticed the rest of the team watching her as they worked at their stations. Finally, Martin said, "Yes, of course, we have much to discuss." The two walked into the office and closed the door.

"You called me four days ago and told me you needed the unit. Well, they sent me to evaluate. What activity are you seeing?"

Martin seized the opportunity to deflect his true nature. "It was this family that was compromised. I believe the mother Jane Stover is a hybrid queen, her husband and son drones, and I think the daughter Molly was murdered. This leaves three other drones, Dr. Brady, Allen Mercer, and Ayaz Arslan."

"Where are they now?" Amy asked as she tried to listen carefully.

"We have lost them, and I fear they knew we were getting close, and they decided to move the queen out of danger."

"So, your investigation is finished here?" Amy asked as she studied every gesture.

Martin paused and said, "I think the worst here is over, and using federal resources at this point would be a waste."

Amy reached for the lamp on the desk and turned the light on as she looked at Martin closely. "I needed that to write," Amy said as she pulled a paper and a pen from her purse. Amy looked at Martin's face, and it revealed nothing unusual. Martin sat back as she wrote and felt relieved that he spent the night feeding and knew he must do so to keep his appearance. Amy handed Martin a slip of paper that had her hotel and room number.

"Olivia and Sanchez are in fourteen, and I am in seventeen. We will stay until the end of the week if you need us; otherwise, if you have any information beyond that time that will help us, just call like you did before." Amy handed Martin a business card as she stood up and walked out of the office. Martin, proud of his act, contemplated sending drones to turn the doctor and the soldiers.

Trixie arrived at the courthouse title office and asked the clerk for any title files for the names on the suspect list. The clerk searched the filing cabinets before returning to the counter.

"I have one title for Stover and Mercer, along with one for Brady, and that is it," the clerk reported. Trixie searched through the titles before the excitement of discovery hit her senses.

"I need to use your phone!" Trixie exclaimed as she pulled out a card from her pants pocket.

Amy arrived back at the hotel as she proceeded to knock on the door of the soldiers. A voice from behind the door said, "The blue clouds are low," for which Amy replied, "I have no lunch money." The door opened to Gonzalez and Olivia dressed in civilian casual clothing.

Amy closed the door and looked at the men, and said, "We have a problem. You need to get ready. I have confirmed Martin and the state investigators have all been turned."

"How do we know for sure?" Gonzalez asked.

"I have a source and set a trap!" Amy said, and she smiled as she closed the door.

Trixie arrived at the cabin and slowly made her way to the front door. Drawing her pistol as she pushed the door open, she was relieved to find nothing but the empty silence and old furniture. Before she could make it too far into the structure, a vehicle approached from the path. Trixie placed her pistol back in its holster as the visitors were revealed.

"Hello again!" she said as Amy, Gonzalez, and Olivia exited the truck. Olivia and Gonzalez broke for the wood line as Amy smiled at Trixie and said, "Are you ready?" Amy grabbed the radio handset from inside the truck and began her contact.

"Martin Donnell, this is Amy. Do you copy?"

Martin's voice came through over a wave of static. "Go ahead," Martin said as Amy laid out her response.

"Martin, we have all the suspects held up in a cabin north of town about ten miles on Old Road one-ten just past the covered bridge. You will see a dirt path leading up the hill to a pond beyond the woods. The cabin is just beyond that. Over."

Martin responded and advised that himself and the team were in route and would arrive shortly. Amy placed the handset back in the truck and motioned Trixie as the two walked toward the cabin. Trixie took a seat on the couch as Amy closed the door behind them and said, "Now we wait!"

The headlights grew brighter in the night as Martin and his team arrived at the path before the cabin. They exited the trucks and drew weapons as the team slowly approached the cabin. Martin noticed the cruiser and the truck and got excited about the prospect of defeating the doctor. Trixie moved to the window and drew her pistol as Amy nodded to her on her way out the front door. Amy said, "Hello Martin," as she stopped short of the edge of the porch. Martin and the team walked closer, standing in the open field under the fall moonlight.

"I am sorry the fake suspects aren't here, but you and your team are. Or should I say you imposters?"

Martin snarled and said, "When did you realize it?"

Amy shrugged and said, "I suspected, and I used what you used to be. Martin and his team nothing more than bait a canary left to die in a dark place, expendable because he had no one to miss him; the rest were all collateral and necessary to bring you out in the open."

Martin smiled as his eyes turned black and his fangs emerged. "We will enjoy eating you both," Martin growled as he motioned his team to advance.

Amy held out her hands and said "Stop! I have one more thing to tell you before you kill us." Martin and the group stopped as Amy said, "Do you smell that? Fuckin' monster, this one is for America and all of the innocent you have destroyed!" Martin stopped as he caught the breeze across the field, and the smell of garlic filled his senses. Amy had a brief flashback in her mind of the day spent dumping barrels of garlic and water over the field as she smiled. Then Amy turned her head and looked toward the dark woods as anticipation made her senses tingle.

Before Martin could make an advance, his head exploded, followed by two more of his team—one after the other. The monsters separated as they ran onto the path and paused at the sound of a high pitch whistle coming from the wood line, which disoriented them as they fell to the ground. Rockets from overhead crashed into the field, exploding, and destroying the *Ubies*. A helicopter rose higher from its cover barely above the tree line as it flew overhead, dropping napalm over the field and turning the area into a blast of flames.

The radio clicked as Amy walked to her truck to grab the handset. The group listened as Amy began to talk. "Good job, Gonzalez, keeping the chopper hidden until the right time."

"Roger that, boss, we got them for sure. This OH-6 always packs the element of surprise, ma'am. I will land beyond the kill box and begin corpse recovery."

Olivia arrived beside Amy, returning from the wood line. "Not my best snipe effort, but this Winchester never fails. Did you see his head explode like a melon? This new ammo is great! Good thing you didn't share that ultrasonic tech with Martin back at Boston. That frequency is out of our range, but it totally fucks them, ma'am!"

Amy smiled and said, "That's why we are going to win this war. They may have our biology—but not our technology." Amy clicked and talked into the handset. "Delta Romeo Charlie, the Alpha is eliminated. Proceed with screaming eagle. Over."

The static broke and a voice replied, "Roger, daughter."

Amy smiled as Olivia said, "Is that your dad—Ruddy? I thought he was missing or dead."

Amy smiled and said, "He has been looking out for his little girl and pulling recon on this area for three weeks. I already knew what was happening here before we arrived."

Trixie shrugged as she looked at the burning field and then the other two. "I still don't know what I just saw or what is happening."

Amy smiled and said, "Well, it's not over yet, and you will be briefed. Welcome to Unit Forty-Seven."

Ruddy carefully leaned on top of the bomb as he signed his name, "With love, forty-seven." Backing off the large device, he turned the crank on the truck as the bomb angle tilted downward. Setting the timer, Ruddy caught a glimpse of himself in the side mirror of the truck long enough to smile with his clean-shaven face and head and say, "God, we look good." Ruddy hustled around to the driver's side and got into the truck before starting the engine and pressing the cable release button.

The bomb slid off the rail and into Martha. Ruddy placed the truck in drive and accelerated down the path and through the woods to the road, counting down as he drove and waited for the explosion. He finally stopped his truck on the road, the last sequence at hand. As the timer display panel in the truck hit zero, Ruddy turned to see the fire shooting out of the hole followed by the ground shaking. The caves deep underground collapsed and were destroyed as Ruddy clicked in and spoke into the handset, "Hive destroyed. No surface damage to report."

Amy turned to Olivia and Trixie and said, "Now we will have to start at the Clark Farm and search for anything that escaped. The rest of the unit has been advised and will meet us there for cleanup." Amy turned to Trixie and said, "Our intel tells us that the Stover's and their accomplices have been spotted in New Orleans. Coming back here would compromise our cover and operation. When we finish here, we are taking a road trip to find and brief them."

Trixie, still confused and shaken from the night's events, said, "What about my life here?"

Amy smiled and said, "You were killed here tonight a result of an underground methane pocket that exploded. Wanda Trickle no longer exists."

Olivia laughed and said, "My name was Rudy Brown, and I was killed in Saigon in seventy-three. Gonzalez, his name is Charles Alverez; he was MIA in seventy-four. We are all dead except for the boss. Welcome to Unit Forty-Seven, home to dead, monster-hunting Patriots!"

Trixie smiled and said, "I have always liked the name Sally."

Amy looked at the two and said, "OK, time to meet up with the rest of the unit and finish this before sunrise." Amy radioed the team, "Meet us at location Zulu for roundup. Over." Gonzalez and Ruddy replied as the group got into the truck, driving down the path past the dying flames in the field with the remains of victory scattered throughout.

HUNGRY MAGGOTS MUST SURVIVE

Dawn broke through the trees as Molly emerged from a hole by the bank of a shallow creek. Her naked, pale body was smeared with earth from her crawl from the depths. She walked to the deeper part of the creek and submerged herself to clean her skin. Looking at her reflection in the still water as she stood up, she realized her skin was translucent and she must feed. She looked up at the sun rise and realized this would not help her. Molly began to walk down the wooded hill as fatigue and hunger built. Her delirium turned her predator self into a bewildered shadow of her killer self.

Molly began to stop at the trees, sliding open her vagina with her fingers as she pissed ammonia. Her head was bobbling back and forth as she continued to walk and piss all the way down the hillside. *I smell like such a hungry maggot*, she thought. At the bottom of the hill, Molly climbed down into the thick brush to hide from the sun and rest. Molly laid curled in the leaves and short grass. The voices in her head of all she had become echoed through her mind. *The beginning*, she thought, *I was the first. I climbed from the water perfect and reborn. Dracula believed in me, and I could not produce. I thought he was the one. I must survive this defeat*, she thought, as Molly's voice spoke, "I hope you die for killing me and making me kill my mother and John." *Get out of my head*, she thought, as she turned and curled her body. The hours passed as Molly slumbered and regained strength and bearing. The night moved in as Molly awoke and continued her exodus. She paused as she arrived at the highway with a bar and service station across the pavement. Her naked body would cause commotion, she thought, but she was too hungry just to walk away. Molly watched for a bit before crossing the road. The bar door opened, and the few patrons noticed her grand entrance. The bartender said "Miss, you need to get some clothes on," while pointing at the "No Shoes, No Shirt, No Shit" sign behind the bar. Molly looked with her innocent blue eyes and said, "But I was abducted and escaped."

The bartender went into a room behind the bar and returned with blanket. He walked up to Molly and threw it over her as he said, "Have a seat, and I will get your information and contact the sheriff!"

Molly said, "Wait, please. I am so hungry. Can you feed me first?" Molly looked at the three men at the bar and back at the bartender. "Please lock the door. My captor may be looking for me!"

The bartender grabbed a shotgun from under the bar and proceeded to lock the door and turn off the "Open" sign. He returned to the other side of the bar, laying the weapon on the counter as he looked at Molly. "You look pale. What would you like to eat?" Molly grabbed the shotgun in one hand, crushing the barrel with her other hand, and threw off the blanket toward the customers as her eyes turned black. She jumped on to the bartender, biting him in the neck as blood sprays covered the row of whiskey bottles and the mirror. She attacked the others one by one. The walls and floor became covered with blood as she ate her way through everyone as they screamed and died. Molly dragged the last and smallest victim, what was left of a little old man, into the restroom. She washed herself in the sink as she pulled the clothes off what was left of the man, washing out the stains and dressing herself.

Molly emerged refreshed and healthy again with a set of keys in her hand. She walked out to the pumps and proceeded to pump fuel on to the lot. Molly checked the vehicles, finding a match in a full conversion van. She started the van. As she climbed in, she pushed in the cigarette lighter to heat, removing the hot plug before throwing it into the path of the gasoline and drove away from the carnage and her defeat as the lot exploded into fire. She looked in the rearview mirror at herself and said, "I wonder if California is nice," before laughing and accelerating into the night.

VENEZUELA

The officers sat across from each other as they sorted through the stack of files. Pausing during the review to sip scotch and ponder the difficult decision they have been tasked with from above. Major Collins read on "The next candidate we have is Sergeant Rutledge Danforth Castle. He joined up in forty-two enlisted as part of the eighty-second served in Sicily, Market Garden, and the bulge. Castle lied about his age to sign up and fight at only sixteen, making him the youngest candidate at twenty-one. He has a wife, Marie Laurent, that he eloped with while serving in France. They have a daughter Amy Marie Castle born last year at Fort Bragg."

The general paused the major with his interruption and said, "he survived all of that hell and still had time to start a family?"

"Yes, Sir. In talking with his commander from his last deployment, they say this kid drinks gasoline and pisses fire!" The major said as he smiled at the general, who remained stone-faced and unamused by the exaggeration.

"Fine then, major, let's bring him in and make our assessment."

The major stood up and walked over to the office door as he opened it to investigate the hallway. Sergeant Castle sat on the bench staring at the floor. The hall echoed as the major cleared his throat, and Castle snapped to attention, producing a perfectly tight salute. The major commanded at ease soldier as he returned the salute. "Please come in; we have much to discuss," as he motioned Castle to follow before leaving the entrance and the door wide open. Castle hustled to the door, snapping his salute one more time to General Morehead. "Please have a seat, soldier" the general said as Castle sat in the empty chair across the desk as the major closed the door and took his place standing behind Castle.

"You are an impressive young Soldier", the general complimented as he looked directly at Castle. "I am not here to jerk at your chin strap;" the general continued "I will get to the point. We have spent days in here and have picked through three hundred files of soldiers just like yourself. We have a delicate mission that requires a certain amount of covert yet aggressiveness if needed. The terrain is littered with enemies but, they too are covert."

"Is it Russia, Sir?" Castle asked as the general paused.

"No soldier, I didn't say I would throw you in a cage with a drunk bear!" The general laughed a bit at his sarcasm as Castle remained nervous and blank. Finally, the general continued with the briefing.

"Venezuela has a host of German ex-pats living and thriving down there. Those German's also include War criminals living among them. We are actively searching for one because he experimented on our men captured and rounded up in secret camps. His name is Dr. Gustav Wagner." The general pulls out a photo from a file and passes it to Castle. Castle studies the photo as the general continues. "I was hoping you could go to Venezuela, find this beast, and bring him back here to Germany so he can stand trial like the others. You will not go in uniform; consider this a vacation. I want you posing as an American on vacation with his family. We have a hotel selected that some of our other selections will secure to keep your wife and daughter safe but, you must keep the appearance as a tourist. You identify the location of Wagner; you visit this man," as the general passes another photo to Castle. "His name is Ernesto Rojas; he has a local clothing store and has been our eyes and ears since before the war. He will communicate through the proper channels notify you when that communication is complete; at that point, you and your family will check out of the hotel.

We will have a small naval vessel docked waiting for your family to board and taken to Aruba, where another ship will take them to Mayport. You will then head by yourself to Rojas clothing store meet up with the others, and we were hoping you could lead the attack and apprehension of Wagner. You will take him to the new airport outside Caracas; we will have a plane waiting to take you, Wagner, and the Team to Mayport, where we will be taking Wagner into custody, and you, your wife, and baby girl will be reunited."

Castle studies the photos and pauses to engage the general. "Why me and my Family, Sir?" The general takes another sip of his scotch as he looks up at Major Collins; still standing behind then looks at Castle directly. "Castle because you have seen the worst of it and survived with savage bravery. You are from Texas, and your mother's maiden name was Anna Maria Ortega. This explains why you had a particular connection with your French wife because of your mother's middle name. I get that but, this means you have Mexican in those veins and could pass as Ernesto's half-white Grandson. Congratulations your cover name is Daniel Allen Rojas. Conveniently your wife and daughter only must change the last name. When this mission is complete, the army will grant you a full honorable discharge and a check for $50,000 courtesy of the war department."

Castle sat up straight from his photo examination and said, "You must want this Wagner awful bad, sir—too much to watch him stand trial and face execution."

The general looked at Major Collins and said, "I knew this soldier was competent when I saw him. Yes, Sergeant, we are interested in the type of experiments he was conducting and need him for his research. The rest is confidential, but do this for America and the army, and we will forever be grateful. This mission could lead to future missions if you are successful. Everything you need is in this envelope," he said as the general passed the material to Castle. "You will be staying at the Hotel Avila Caracas while meeting up with your grandpa. Is that OK with you, Mr. Rojas?"

Castle nodded and said, "Yes, sir, I never shrink from a challenge, and if you think I am tough, you haven't met my wife. She was part of the resistance in Paris, where we met after liberation."

"It sounds like you two are a match made in heaven," the general said as he placed his hands on the desk.

The general stood up as Castle snapped to his feet. The two soldiers saluted one another. Castle made his way through the open door made possible by Major Collins and continued his range walk down the hall.

"Do you think he will make it?" Collins asked the general as he closed the door.

The general shook his head and said, "Hopefully but the other twelve men were just as brave or stupid and all ended up missing."

―

Castle rested poolside, watching the rest of the guests from behind his sunglasses. He turned his attention to his wife and daughter playing in the water. *I am glad she decided to go along with this*, he thought. She had lived with lies before in Paris when the Nazis had control. She hated Nazis after what they did to her parents and sister.

That was why she was here. She wanted revenge for them. Revenge can be a great motivation, Castle thought as he watched his wife. She was playing the part perfectly—the wife of Daniel Rojas. Castle shook his head as he got up from the lounge chair and walked over to his wife.

"Marie, my love, I have some errands to run and will meet you back at the room later."

Marie looked up at her husband with their daughter in her arms and said, *"D'accord et au revoir."* Castle smiled as he loved her French even when she told him goodbye. He walked away from the pool with his yellow shirt unbuttoned, collar sticking up, finished off with black shorts and sandals. Projecting this tourist vibe, he thought as he made his way from the hotel grounds to the street. Walking helped him keep a low profile, he reasoned, as he thought, If I had picked a better pair of shoes, looking down at his cheap sandals. Castle stopped and removed the sandals from his feet one by one and used the shade of the buildings to walk on the cool pavement. The distance was nothing compared to the march across Europe. Castle stopped at a stand, placing his sandals back on his feet, as the downtown was no longer present to provide shade from the heat.

"Quisiera un papel por favor." The general was right; his mother and her heritage served him well. He grabbed the paper and paid the twenty *centimos*. "Gracias!" he said as he walked on, making his way to a wooden bench on the corner of the intersection. Castle looked at the home over the top of the paper. He marveled at its size but made notice of its perimeter fence, guards, and dogs that he could count in between the iron bars. He continued to watch as he filtered through the paper, reading what pieces of the dialect he could remember. The day wore on as Castle made his way from the bench to a local restaurant at the opposite end of the street but still viewed the house. He rested at a table on the walk

with the shade of an umbrella to block the sunlight. He removed his glasses and looked around the bar as the waiter came to take his order. He ordered his tacos and beer while quietly studying the crowd. His ear caught a piece of the German language as he slowly turned his head to look over his right shoulder. He saw three men surrounding a man seated in the center.

The conversation between them and the fact that he was not fluent in German made it hard to follow. The men were all dressed in white suits topped off with fedoras and sunglasses. The man at the center was Wagner. Castle relaxed back in his seat and turned his attention toward his food as he tried to maintain a casual manner not to arouse suspicion. Castle continued to dine and drink as the men he watched passed by his table, crossing the street to the house. After finishing the last bit of beer, Castle left the money on the table, grabbed his paper, and walked downtown.

Arriving at the clothing store—*Palacio de la Ropa* the sign read—Castle entered the small shop as a bell chimed announcing his entrance. Ernesto stood behind the counter folding pants.

"Grandpa! It's me, Daniel," he said as he committed to his character for the other patrons.

Ernesto put down the pants and walked behind the counter and hugged Castle, whispering in his ear, "Follow me," as he turned to his helper. "Pablo, please watch the store. I am taking my grandson to the back to catch up." Pablo nodded as he watched the two men leave the floor and vanish behind a door leading to the stock room.

Ernesto walked to a wooden shelf lined with shoes and pulled on the center as the shelf swung open. The two men entered a hallway as Ernesto pulled the frame closed behind them. They walked down the hall leading to a flight of stairs, went down the stairs, and reached a metal door. Ernesto produced a key and unlocked the door, inviting Castle to enter as he closed another door behind them. The room was small and lined with maps on the wall, and a large radio broadcasted a low hum of chatter and static.

Ernesto turned to Castle and said, "I assume you found him."

Castle nodded said, "Affirmative, sir, I have been canvassing the city for weeks and finally yesterday caught a lead. I was at a local market and noticed a German woman shopping. That is nothing unusual as this place is loaded with Kraut, but the clerk was also German, and the only thing I could pick up was 'to give my best to Wagner.' So, I followed the woman out of the market, leading me to a large house compound about ten blocks north. Here is the location," as Castle points at a map on the wall.

"The house looks heavily secured and full of guards."

Ernesto smiled and said, "Good work. Maybe now I can go back to Chicago."

Castle shrugged and said, "You are not from here?"

"Hell no!" Ernesto replied in perfect English. "I am from the eastside, brother. I have been down here since thirty-six. I am as American as apple pie and baseball. My grandparents immigrated from Mexico, and my dad married an immigrant from Puerto Rico." The two men laugh at one another as Ernesto said, "By the way, my name is Ernie. I will send the message to command. Wait for communication at the hotel green lighting the next phase, and we will assemble here soon."

The two men walked back through the door and stepped to the shop floor. Castle looked at Ernie and said, "Thank you for the money, Grandpa," as he waved and left the shop.

The journey back to the hotel as the evening approached left Castle determined as it gave him time to work his attack strategy in his mind. For example, if I blast the gate draw out, the guards and dogs set up a kill box while someone sneaks in the fence from the rear and into the house, quickly and quietly grabbing the target, then walk right out the front door to a waiting vehicle and off to the airport we go.

His plan faded as he entered his room to see his wife and daughter sleeping on the bed. "Marie," he said as he nudged her, "it's time." Marie sat up slowly as to not wake the baby, smiled at her husband, and kissed his forehead before moving about the room, gathering up and packing possessions. The time was short as the phone rang out. Castle picked up the receiver; the voice on the other end confirmed that a paper message was waiting at the front desk. Castle nodded at his wife as he hung up the receiver and grabbed the suitcases. His wife picked up their daughter and exited the room.

They made it to the lobby as Castle retrieved the message and checked out. The three walked out the front as Castle whistled for a taxi. Castle opened the trunk, placing the baggage inside before joining his wife and daughter in the back seat. Castle read the message and told the driver to drive to *Port de Plaisance* as he handed the driver a role of American dollars. The driver stepped on the accelerator, excited by the exchange. Castle put his arm around his wife and daughter. The ride was long as they left the city and arrived at the dock.

Castle thanked the driver with another role of dollars before leaving the car with his family and removing the belongings from the trunk. He walked Marie and Amy to pier twenty as the navy ship awaited. He turned to see the captain and another man walking down the ramp to greet him. "Sergeant," the captain said, "this is Stanley Jackson; he will take your bags and take good care of your wife and daughter."

"If you would like to come with me, ma'am," the captain said as he motioned them before Jackson picked up the bags.

Marie kissed Castle on the lips as he rubbed Amy on the head. They followed the captain onto the ship as the mates unhooked from the ramp, and the boat began to move away as the engine gained power. Castle returned to the taxi as he passed the new destination on to the driver. Castle looked out the window into the night as he rested his mind and concern over his family and shifted his thoughts toward the task ahead before closing his eyes. The taxi stopped as the brakes' squeaks alerted Castle to open his eyes and raise his head. The taxi parked in front of the clothing store as Castle exited before supplying the driver with one last roll of dollar bills and one last parting "thanks." The driver smiled as he left Castle standing on the curb.

Castle turned and walked to the front door of the store, slowly turning the knob to enter. Closing the door behind him, Castle noticed a dim light coming from the stock room. He walked through the store behind the counter toward the light. In the stock room, he was greeted by three men seated around a small table. Ernie looked at Castle and said, "Did everything go as planned?"

Castle replied, "So far. Now let's finish this."

Ernie smiled and said, "OK, take a seat, and meet the rest of the team."

Castle moved to the table and occupied the empty chair. He looked at new faces and said, "I am Sergeant Castle."

The first man to speak said, "We know you and have been briefed. We kept a low profile as guests at the hotel and made sure you and your family were not harmed. I am Agent Torres, and this is Agent Sanchez of the CIA; we are your direct support. There is currently a military coup plot being monitored by our government. We were pulled from that detail to assist you."

"What is the CIA?" Castle said as he looked at the two men.

Torres replied, "It is a new government agency created last month, and it stands for Central Intelligence Agency."

Sanchez spoke up and said, "The world is changing, and we are along with it. We have been set up primarily to prevent the rise of Communism and other foreign threats through subversive tactics. We were both selected for this mission for some of the same reasons you were. But, unlike you, these are our real names."

Torres smiled as he said, "You have an impressive combat resume. How do you think we should proceed?"

Castle leaned forward and began to lay out his plan. "The situation is there are four of us and probably ten or more guards, by my best count. We need a truck, weapons, and explosives. Ernie, you will be the driver. You will circle once stop just beyond the restaurant at the next block. Then, as you come around again, stop at the corner by the bench and wait. When that happens, one of us bombs the gate while another lays down suppressive fire. This will provide enough distraction for one of us to sneak in over the brick wall where the fence ends and grab the target. By that time, most guards should be eliminated, and we can walk the target right out the front door."

Torres looked at Castle and said, "We will take the front if you feel comfortable apprehending the target."

Ernie smiled as he listened and said, "You can't go in those outfits. You all look like a Mexican mariachi band waiting to entertain on a cruise ship. I have black uniforms in the radio room that I borrowed from the local communists. Make sure you change those sandals. I can't have my grandson tripping over his own feet." Ernie laughed as he stood up from the table. "When you are finished, meet me out back!" Ernie instructed as he walked toward the exit.

The men left the table and walked single file through the remainder of the stock room and toward the radio room. Moments later they emerged from the back door, arriving at a box truck. Ernie finished off a cigarette, flicking it into the alley, as he said, "That is more like it," as he looks the men from head to toe. Ernie walked to the truck's rear as he opened the doors and said, "Here is what we have, the courtesy of our friends at the war department!" The men investigated the trailer stocked with rifles, ammunition, flare supplies, and crates of grenades.

Torres said, "One more thing. If we get separated, the rally point is the dock where you dropped off your family—but instead, pier twenty-five. The location is also our escape if the mission fails. We have a fishing boat waiting with instructions secured in the cabin overhead storage bin. We cannot leave anyone behind and must hold until either we retrieve each other, or we all make it through this and report. If no one has any questions, let's get this mission completed."

The three men got in the back of the truck utilizing a series of lanterns to light the space as Ernie shut the doors and made his way to the driver's seat. The box truck began to move as the men prepared. They armed up and discussed tactics. The vehicle shook and vibrated as the men kept steady as they worked. Finally, Ernie stopped the truck and stepped out to open the doors. The three men got out as Torres and Sanchez moved into the restaurant's garden and held the position. The two agents watched as Castle made his way down the street, and Ernie closed the doors, then continued to drive the truck on the designated path. Castle made his way where the fence turned to the wall, and low crawled into position. The agents waited until they saw Ernie stop with the truck up the street. Sanchez pulled a grenade from a bag as Torres locked his rifle and assumed a prone position facing the gate. Sanchez pulled the pin and threw the grenade as it sailed in the air, bouncing off the street and landing short of the gate. He grabbed a second and threw just as the first one exploded, sending smoke and debris in all directions. The second landed just inside the entrance as another explosion forced an opening. Guards exited the compound as Torres began to engage.

Sanchez grabbed his rifle, moved away from Torres, and fired at the guards as they gathered position and returned fire. Castle slung his rifle and climbed the wall. Jumping down off the wall, he set position on one knee and scanned, looking down his sight at the backyard for any guards. He ran to the back door, stopping to smash the handle and lock with the butt of his rifle. Entering the kitchen, he crouched down by the counter to pause for any aggressors.

He heard movement over his shoulder as he stood, took aim, and shot, and a guard fell to the floor. Castle stood and moved through the dark house, aiming as he went. He turned another corner by the staircase and caught sight of two men and Gustav as they moved out of sight. Castle turned and ran down the short hallway to intercept. He turned to find a closed door at the end. He backed up and shot at the door several times before turning the knob.

A guard fell to the floor as the door opened. Castle stepped over the man as he stepped through the doorway and a first in a series of steps leading down into darkness. Castle grabbed a flare gun from his belt and shot the flare down into the room. The area turned red, revealing a tunnel entrance in the basement wall. Castle sighted his rifle on the tunnel as he moved forward. As he was moving toward the bottom of the stairs, Castle sighted around the room as the flare faded. Grabbing his lighter from his pocket and determined to complete the mission, Castle slowly made his way into the tunnel. The lighter supplied only dim light as the tunnel appeared straight. Castle closed the lighter, extinguishing the light and opting to feel his way to avoid detection. Finally, he noticed the light ahead. The light from the moon revealed an open gate leading out to the top of a wooded slope. Castle slowly exited the tunnel. Before he could react, he was hit from behind and knocked unconscious.

FERTILE DIRT STUDIO

The first sense to return was hearing accompanied by a headache. Castle remained still with his eyes closed and finally tried to listen for sounds around him, a whisper. "Buddy, hey, Mack, are you awake? Hello, come on, possum, that shit will not work." Castle opened his eyes and noticed he was in a large cell. He sat up and looked toward the source of the whisper to see a man sitting in a bathrobe and slippers on a bed. Castle looked around the cell, trying to gather his location.

The walls were smooth stone and the floor concrete, and the bars were thick iron. The man said, "I am Lieutenant Oliver Warner. My friends call me Ollie."

Castle looked back at the man and said, "Where the hell are we?"

Ollie said, "Well, that's easy; we are in a cave trapped in hell. Now, what's your name?"

"Where are you From Ollie?" Castle asked as he rubbed the back of his neck.

"Jersey-born and army raised," Ollie said as he nodded.

Castle said, "Should I salute?"

"No," Ollie said. "What I meant to say is I was a lieutenant. Sorry, just excited to have someone to talk too. I had a bad landing in Italy from a jump and broke my arm. I was sent back home, where they put pins in my arm and gave me a desk job doing requisition for deployment in the war department. I reported to General Moorhead. that is how I ended up here."

"Moorhead? what do you mean?" Castle said as he continued to rub his neck.

"Moorhead promised me $100,000 to come down here and pretend to be a businessman to look for some criminal named Gustav." Castle raised his head and looked at Ollie as he became angry. Ollie shook his head and said, "He must have got you too? We aren't the only ones; there were at least ten that I can count."

"Ten!" Castle said, "Where are they?"

Ollie said, "I am pretty sure all dead from what I saw. See, we are in a cave. I almost escaped last week; down the hall is where the bunker ends and the cave starts. Beyond the door is an underground river that feeds to the hillside of the mountain we are in. I made it that far before getting caught by some powerful guards. I was awake when they first brought me here. A road leads up to this mountain; we are only about ten minutes west of Caracas. I only know this because I used the sun and counted in my head."

"Have you given them any information?" Castle said.

"Information about what? They don't want the information. We are experiments," Ollie said.

"My name is Sergeant Rutledge Danforth Castle; now tell me more!"

Ollie said, "Well, that's too much; how about we call you Ruddy." Ruddy thought of his Father and nodded as Ollie continued. "I have been here for a while. The last guy was the one who told me about the exit before he was gone."

Ollie pulled up his robe and exposed his penis, red and bloody, as Ruddy said, "What the hell!"

"It's sex, Ruddy! Nonstop sex! There is this German woman. She is a tall, blond, and strong. Her skin is like milk, but in her eyes—something is wrong with her eyes. I think she is a Nazi experiment. She wants to get pregnant. One by one, she has tried all men that have been here, including me. She squeezed my bad arm so hard our last time I think it might be broken again." Ollie rolled up his sleeve as he showed his swollen arm and the scar from his surgery while his penis remained on display.

Ruddy said, "OK, I get it. Do you mind putting that away?"

Ollie said, "Sure," while he rolled his sleeve down and left his bloody cock dangling about.

FERTILE DIRT STUDIO

Ollie said "I am done soon; they will kill me, and then it will be your turn. The guy that runs this place, his name is Gunther. The guards patrol the upper level from the cave to the mountain. I have a bit of linguistic training, and the woman was speaking Turkish. They were talking about an army base underground, I think. Because she said she has a large army."

Ruddy sat back against the wall and closed his eyes as Ollie continued to talk.

The one-way conversation lasted for hours as Ollie started from his childhood forward. Ruddy could tell Ollie was scared as he listened. For a good reason—if what he said was true, then this would mean both their lives. Ruddy thought about his wife and daughter and what he would do to the general if he ever saw him again. Then, finally, Ruddy heard a noise as the door opened down the hall and a man entered carrying two food trays. The man stopped in front of the cell, looked at Ruddy, and said, "I am glad you are awake. I am sure our other guest has told you everything, but don't worry. If you do what we say, you will get along just fine."

"This tall Nazi asshole is Gunther!" Ollie said to Ruddy as he shook his head and pointed. He got up off his bed and grabbed the trays being passed through a slot in the door.

Gunther said, "I thank you and the Fourth Reich thanks you. Now eat, gentlemen. Get your strength; you will need it." Gunther snapped his boots together as his decorated uniform and demeanor made him appear dated and theatrical. Ruddy shook his head and sighed as he watched him march away from the cell.

Ruddy took the tray from Ollie and began to eat as his mind began working on a plan of escape. Ollie finished quickly as he laid the tray on the floor before lying down on his bed. Ruddy finished as the door opened again, and the woman made her way to the cell flanked by two large armed guards. Her hair was long and blond. Her eyes were clear blue dotted on her pale complexion. She looked at Ollie as he rested and said, "Oliver, it's time!" One guard unlocked the door as the other guard kept his rifle placed at the ready. The woman walked into the cell and nudged Ollie.

Ollie began to cry and scream. "I need rest; I can't take it anymore!"

Ruddy stood in defense as the woman reached out and grabbed him by the throat without making eye contact and said, "It's not your turn!"

Ruddy choked as she squeezed with tremendous strength. Ollie finally stood up and said, "Leave him alone. I will go!" The woman released Ruddy as he struggled to breathe. Ollie looked back at Ruddy as he was rushed out of the cell, and the door slammed and locked behind him. Ruddy laid back down on the bed and rested to save his strength. *The woman wasn't afraid*, he thought. The guards were armed and could have easily entered the cell and taken Ollie, yet she did it. Ruddy rested on the bed, drifting in and out of sleep for what felt like a lifetime. Finally, the door opened again, and Ruddy looked up to see the return of Ollie.

What he saw shook even his rugged nature. The woman was naked, covered in blood and dragging what was left of Ollie behind her. The guards followed the trail of blood and moved around the woman to unlock the cell door. The woman opened the cell and threw the body on the floor with little effort. She looked at Ruddy with her blackened eyes and said, "This is what lack of cooperation gets you! I will leave this here as a reminder! You had better think about this because tomorrow you and I begin!" Ruddy lowered his head in shock as he couldn't bring himself to look at the bloody mess anymore. He listened as the cell door closed and then heard the closing of the hallway door.

I can't go like this, he thought. *I won't go like this. I must think of a way out of here now!*

Ruddy stood up and walked to the body to look for dog tags to take with him, keeping his optimism and fight alive. He reached for the neck, finding the tags, as he looked at the bite marks and thought it must have been a wild animal. *Why was she covered in blood?* Ruddy thought. Maybe she is a demon, he concluded. Ruddy wiped the blood off the tags and read the information before placing them in his pocket.

He looked down one more time and noticed a metallic shine coming from the body. Ruddy bent down to examine, seeing a series of pins in what was left of the arm. Then he remembered what Ollie had told him. Ruddy grabbed the tags from his pocket and used the edge and his other hand to dig the pins from the broken arm. He then took the tags to sharpen the longest pin he could salvage to fashion a weapon before looking at the lock. Ruddy slowly looked over to the cell door and at the empty hall as he slid the pin around the mechanism. Sliding the pin into the lock, he pushed and shook until the lock opened. Ruddy slowly opened the door and ran to the next door. He used the pin again to pick the next lock as he opened the door.

Ruddy crouched down and slowly closed it. He slowly moved at the base of the wall before turning to see the water flowing and draining into a hole. The cave was deep with light peeking through from the very top. Ruddy caught a glimpse of two guards heading his way as he quietly climbed in the pool of water, diving as deep as he could to submerge himself, and held his breath. The current pulled him until he was in the hole. Ruddy saw the opening and could stop himself long enough to catch his breath. He decided to stay with the water instead of climbing out of the space.

Ruddy let go of the wall as the current pulled him further along. He slid deeper until finally shooting out a rock wall and falling into the river below. Ruddy began to swim with the current as he turned to look at the mountain and the road that made a path to the cave. His anger and adrenaline kept him moving as he continued to hurry with the current.

Torres and Ernie sat in the cabin of the boat as Sanchez pulled security. "What are we going to tell his wife?" Ernie said.

"The general will be happy that we got the files he wanted and could get those flown out. As far as Gustav goes, he will for sure try harder to hide. We will be lucky if he surfaces again. Sergeant Castle was a good soldier, and we have waited three days; we will have to cut our losses and consider this mission completed. We will let the army handle his wife!"

The two men continued to talk as they planned to prepare for departure. Sanchez began to holler as the two men surfaced on deck. The three men saw Ruddy approaching slowly down the pier. His limp was noticeable; his body was hunched as he held his side; his appearance was muddied, ragged, and concerning as Torres jumped off the deck and ran to Ruddy.

"Damn soldier, you made it! We looked everywhere for you! We found your weapon outside the tunnel and lost the trail a mile in."

Ruddy stopped and looked at Torres and said, "The mission is not over!"

Torres looked Ruddy in the eyes and said, "Yes, we didn't get Gustav but got his files; we were holding hope for you. Command says we are to depart and return home. We can't stay any longer; that house we raided has caused focus and tension with the police and government."

FERTILE DIRT STUDIO

Ernie and Sanchez approached as Ruddy said, "I escaped a Nazi camp in the jungle, lost a friend, floated down river to escape torture, and walked fifteen miles to get here. I want some payback!"

The men looked at each other and nodded as Ernie said, "We can't turn our back on evil."

"I need a favor!" Ruddy said. "I need a bomb and a truck!"

Ernie smiled and said, "I know just the man to contact. You may know him!"

General Moorhead sat at his desk reading the newspaper when there was a knock at his door. The general said, "Come in!" and smiled at the entrance of Ruddy. Ruddy saluted as the general reached for a handshake. "Please sit down, soldier; we have much to talk about," the general said as he returned to his seat. Ruddy sat as the general said, "I read the report from the team you were with, and they told me you performed exceedingly well!"

Ruddy said, "It was a high cost and not a complete success. We lost too many good men that you sent before me, including Oliver Warner! Gustav got away, but the files were recovered. The Nazi bunker in the cave was destroyed by the bomb you sent. I mounted it on the back of a truck. I signed a thank-you to Oliver for saving my life and placed my name on it before dropping it into the cave. We were able to deny our involvement at Gustav's home and the explosion at the mountain by blaming it on the military coup. I will expose all of this unless you do the right thing!"

"What is that precisely?" the general said as he leaned forward.

Ruddy said, "I want $100,000 paid to all the families of the soldiers that went down there and died before me. That includes my family and my team."

The general smiled and said, "What do I get in return?"

Ruddy said, "The team that I worked with down there, along with myself, will form a secret unit. I want to call this Unit Forty-Seven in memory of those other soldiers. I want to hunt whatever that was that I detailed in my report and things like it, all the while keeping a low profile separate from other agencies."

"You find me proof of what is in that report and whatever unexplained activity you encounter," the general said as he smiled at Ruddy. "I want you to operate from Wright Patterson as I have been holding on to this newspaper, waiting for you to return for the next mission."

The general handed Ruddy the paper, and he read the headline. He looked at the general and said, "What does this Roswell business have to do with Wright Patterson?"

"That's where they took the bodies, and I was hoping you could compare what you saw with these things. We have the threat of Russia, aliens, and whatever was in your report to contend with. I am sure you and your team are up to the challenge. What is this business about Turkey?"

"Oliver told me a secret army was mentioned during his time in lock-up—something about a Fourth Reich."

"Look, I know his death was terrible by all accounts in your report; he got fucked to death. This Gunther you mention in your report, no one has ever heard of him, and the blond without a name is no use to us. I am back here in DC, which means it will be easier to get things done. You are dismissed and keep me posted directly on your progress!"

Ruddy stood up and saluted as the general stood to walk behind him and watched him walk down the hall before closing the door.

The general sat back in his chair as he thought to himself, *At least I got the files.* That information on us could have been very damaging. Those files were worth the price paid. I can't just kill him; it would be too suspicious. He wasn't supposed to survive. I can steer his direction as I have his trust. The queen must start over now that Venezuela is destroyed, and the loss of Gunther does little harm. This war has helped our discretion. If man continues to kill each other through war and disagreements, we can hide right under their nose; Ohio would be perfect. Let him waste some time chasing aliens. Humans are so kept with the heavens and technology that they are unaware of what is right in front of them. Let him go to Turkey; my queen hasn't been there for hundreds of years. He returns with proof; we call him crazy and continue to operate as we have for centuries.

The general smiled as his eyes turned black, and his fangs gave way to his true nature.

Ruddy looked back at the large brick complex as he walked down the steps and into the cool fall day. He noticed Ernie, Sanchez, and Torres next to Marie and Amy standing on the curb by a car. Ruddy approached, giving Marie a kiss on the lips as he picked Amy up and said, "I am so glad you are walking! You are strong and smart just like your mother!" Ruddy handed Amy to Marie as he looked at the three men and said, "We have got most of what we wanted."

Ernie smiled and said, "You did good, my grandson!" as the team laughed. "I must tell you; it has been an adventure, but I am done with working for the government. I want to thank you all and mean that, but I haven't been home in eleven years and Chicago calls," Ernie said as he crossed his arms.

Ruddy nodded and said, "What will you do with yourself?" Ernie shrugged and said, "I don't know, maybe a bar named Pappy's?" as he began to walk away, waving at the group.

Torres looked at Ruddy and said, "What is the mission?"

Ruddy smiled and said, "Unit Forty-Seven has been reassigned to Wright Patterson for top secret research."

Sanchez shrugged and said, "I have never been to Ohio. What could be so top secret about that?"

Ruddy leaned in closer to both men and said, "Aliens!" The two men laughed as Marie shook her head while placing Amy into the car.

Torres said, "What the general orders and what we do don't have to line up. The general was content sending soldiers to their death over a war criminal and some files!"

"Did anyone look at the files?" Ruddy said as he watched Marie sit in the passenger's seat of the car.

Sanchez said, "I tried but couldn't read the German. All I know is whatever was contained in those files was important to the general. Important enough to make us all expendable!"

Torres said, "What about this German woman? She still must be out there. I say we set up our office in Ohio and begin to quietly dig around on our own and see what we can find out. If we provide the general with generic reports, he will continue to fund our efforts. We owe it to ourselves to search for the truth."

Ruddy walked to the rear fender of his car, stopping short of the driver's seat. He looked at both men, who were still standing on the curb waiting for his decision. He smiled as he looked in the window at his daughter and wife before looking back at the men.

"I have done nothing but think about Ollie since I have been home. He sacrificed his life to save me from certain death. I do not blame Ernie for wanting out of this mess. But, for me, I am in it now, and I owe it to Ollie to find whatever that was that took his life. It was evil, pure evil, and if I turn my back on evil, it will be a mistake. We learned that lesson from this war, staying out of the fight for so long cost so much. I ask myself what I will do if I don't stand and fight. I ask myself, 'Do I still have it in me?' Then I look at my wife and daughter and think, For them I must!"

THE END...FOR NOW

Milton Keynes UK
Ingram Content Group UK Ltd.
UKHW022327030324
438776UK00014B/2196